RESCUE

**Can he save his brother from a
life of hell?**

Leaving home is the only way Thad and his brother Danny can be free from their abusive and overbearing parents. Working long hours and saving every penny he earns is worth it if they can both just live.

But eight months later, Danny's freedom is in jeopardy when his parents want to place him in a conversion therapy camp. Feeling powerless, Thad is left with no choice but to file for custody of his brother.

Jay Dawson knows how it feels not to be wanted by your parents. Despite being shuffled to twenty-two foster homes, his rough start in life didn't hold him back. Now a lawyer, he works with LGBTQ charities to help support kids in and out of the foster system.

When he comes across Thad's case, Jay instantly agrees to represent him in order to protect Danny. Working closely together, the two find a relationship blossoms despite their efforts to avoid it. They discover just how evil Thad's parents truly are when Danny is kidnapped.

Will the lawyer help him save his brother, and maybe discover true love in the end?

RESCUE

FROM THE EDGE

BOOK FOUR

BY EVIE RILEY

Rescue

From The Edge

Book Four

Copyright © 2022

Evie Riley

Second Edition

ISBN: 978-1-77357-695-4

Published by Naughty Nights Press LLC

Cover Art By Willsin Rowe

CHAPTER ONE

Thad

GOD DAMN IT.

This was not a good start to the evening. I was running late, close to thirty minutes now, and I already knew my parents were going to be pissed at me over it. It was bad enough they were already going to be annoyed by my presence. I wasn't looking to make it worse, but apparently the stars were not aligned with me tonight.

At the age of nineteen you would think I wouldn't be so worried about what my parents thought, but I wasn't worried about me. It was my kid brother, Danny, that held all of my concern. Growing up with very religious and strict parents was never easy, but it got increasingly dangerous when you were gay. Luckily for me, I didn't figure out my attraction to guys until recently. Danny, though, he hadn't been so lucky. He knew when he was twelve that he was gay. He kept it hidden, even from me, until he was fourteen.

I could still remember the night he told me as clear as day. I was seventeen and had been working a lot to save up for my own place. I wanted out of that house the moment I legally could. It was late and I heard him crying in his room. I wasn't about to walk away when I could tell he was in pain. That was never something we did with each other. Whenever we needed each other, the other was there.

No questions asked.

Growing up in a very strict home made us rely on each other for basic needs like comfort and love. Whenever one of us had a nightmare, we would go to the other. Whenever we were sick, the other one took care of them.

I was the one that walked him to and from school. I was the one that gave him baths. I was the one that would sneak him food when he didn't like whatever fancy crap our mother cooked. It was him and me against the world and I wouldn't change that.

Yes, it would have made my life easier if I hadn't had to practically raise my kid brother since I was eight, but he was my kid brother and I loved him. I wanted the best for him. It was just that simple.

So, when he was crying in his room, I instantly went in to see what had happened, what had upset him. He was a complete mess and hysterical from emotional pain.

It was that night that I discovered he was gay.

He was upset because our father had gone on a long rant about a gay guy he'd seen at church. He called the guy horrible names and those words cut deep in Danny.

I knew our parents would never accept him, they would do anything they could to force Danny to keep it hidden and to be straight. To me, though, I just wanted him happy. I didn't care who he loved as long as he got to experience it.

That night, I knew I wouldn't be able to leave him behind when I left. I started working even more to save up more so I could afford a two bedroom apartment. Once I turned eighteen, I moved out and Danny followed behind me six weeks later when he came out to our parents. They didn't handle it well and they kicked him out. That was eight months ago, and they had never reached out to him since.

I hadn't been so lucky.

They called every week to see if I had managed to convince my brother that he wasn't gay. They believed it was a phase or a hormone imbalance that was causing him to feel the way that he did.

They had no idea.

To them, being attracted to the same sex was a mistake and God couldn't possibly make a mistake like that.

They would never accept him.

They would never accept me.

They didn't know I was gay.

I hadn't told anyone, not even Danny. It wasn't that I thought he wouldn't be okay with it, obviously he would be. It was more about me. I wasn't really ready to admit it out loud just yet. I was still adjusting to it all. Adjusting to my new reality and the new piece of myself.

Growing up, I had never looked at another guy like that before. Changing and showering in the locker room was nothing to me. I still didn't understand why all of a sudden I started checking out guys and watching gay porn.

I had started watching porn when I was seventeen, like most teenagers do, but it was always straight or girl on girl. The *typical guy* porn. The thing was, it never got me aroused. It was as if I watched a documentary on frogs or something. I chalked it up to not finding anything that interested me.

It wasn't until six weeks ago when I was feeling horny did I decide to try porn again. I just so happened to pick one that had a threesome with two guys. They were interacting with each other and, for the first time, I was able to orgasm while watching porn. The problem, though, I was busy watching the two guys and not the girl. That started to open up some questions, questions I was still dealing with. I could accept that I was gay. That wasn't too much of a big deal to me.

The problem was, I had no idea what to do about it. It was bad enough when I thought I was straight. I had been confused and self-conscious enough about sex when it was with a woman. I was nineteen and not only still a virgin, but I had never even been kissed.

My parents never allowed me to be alone with a girl. I had dated a couple in the past before I moved out, but I was always supervised. They believed that your first kiss should be at the altar. Now, I was a nineteen year old gold star virgin who was gay. It was a whole other world and I had no idea how to do any of it or how it would make me feel.

Was I a top or was I a bottom?

How would I know?

RESCUE

What would I do if I didn't like giving oral sex or if I didn't want to be a bottom and the guy I was with was a top?

It was so much more complicated and I still wasn't ready to be active on it.

I let out a sigh as I parked in my parents' driveway. I wished I could have just turned around and gone home. I was exhausted from working so many hours this week.

I worked eighty hours every week, on average, just to be able to afford the apartment and have some money saved up for Danny's college education. He would have to get student loans as well, but at least he would have something that he could put toward it.

He wasn't sure what he wanted to do yet, but he was certain he didn't want to be a mechanic, like me. He wasn't interested in working with his hands and he wasn't very good at it, either. He was more book smart than street smart, but that was okay. He deserved to go off to college and I wanted that for him. Even if that meant I worked more hours than I slept in the week.

My parents hated that I was a mechanic. They always had. Ever since I was little, I'd loved cars and being around them. I loved taking mechanical things apart and putting them back together. I used to do it all the time with the lawn mower. It drove them crazy, but I was always able to put it back together.

When I turned sixteen I used some of my money that I had saved up and bought this clunker of a car. My parents hated the thing and made me hide it in the garage so none of the neighbors would see it. I loved it, though, because I could spend all of my free time fixing it up and cleaning it. I had rebuilt the whole engine from parts I was able to pick up. To this day, I still drove it and you would never believe it was the same car.

When a position came up at one of two mechanic shops in town, I quickly grabbed it up and I'd never regretted it since. To my parents, though, I was a disgusting working class citizen. I was less of a man and person because I worked with my hands serving others. To them, I belittled myself because I choose to not work in an office like they did. It didn't matter to me, though. I loved it and I never wanted to do anything else. I hoped one day I could open my own shop and run my own business.

Climbing out of my beloved car, I headed toward the door. I just needed to get this over and done with and then I could go home and relax with Danny. I knocked and waited for one of them to answer the door.

You would think with this being my parents' house that I could just walk right in, but I couldn't. I wasn't allowed to do that, because they found it disrespectful. As a guest, son or not, you waited until you were granted permission to enter the home. It was ridiculous, because I shouldn't be classified as a guest.

I was their son.

I should be able to walk right in.

With that being said, though, they were not allowed to just walk right into my apartment. But that wasn't because I wanted to be rude and make them feel like they had no control of the situation. It was because I worried they would try to grab Danny if they could come in whenever they wanted. I had gone out of my way to ensure that Danny felt safe at home and I was not about to jeopardize that.

The front door opened and my mother stood on the other side. She wore her perfectly ironed sundress with the matching kitten heels. Her hair and makeup were done as if she was going out to church instead of just having dinner at the house. She looked me up and down and I could tell she was disgusted by what she saw. I wore my work clothes so there was black grease on my pants. I had wanted to go home to change before coming over, but I had lost track of time working on a car and didn't have the chance to. At least, I had managed to get the grease off my hands.

"Hello, mother." Always *mother*, never mom. Just like it was always *father* and never dad. To them, anything less would be disrespectful.

"You couldn't have at least bothered to change?"

"I was working late and I didn't want to be any later than I already was. It's dry, it's not going to rub off on anything, mother."

That was another thing we were never allowed to do growing up, get anything dirty. Everything was always pristine. It had to be perfect in case anyone were to surprise us by coming by. It wasn't easy when you had two boys running around.

RESCUE

We always had to be hyper vigilant with what we were doing outside. We couldn't play football after it rained, because if we dragged even a speck of mud into the house, we were stuck scrubbing the floors for hours until our mother was satisfied.

Always having to have the house immaculate growing up was why my apartment looked lived in. It wasn't dirty or messy, but when you walked in you knew people lived there. There was always a coat hanging over the back of a chair and there were dishes in the sink from breakfast. It was lived in and that was exactly how I liked it.

She let out a huff before she moved back and granted me permission to enter. I walked in and instantly removed my boots as she closed the door. There were no hugs or a kiss on the cheek. She would never allow it with me having dirt on my clothes. Even though it was dry and wouldn't transfer, she would never take that risk.

"Dinner is ready," she simply said as she turned on her kitten heels and headed off for the formal dining room.

I couldn't stifle the eye roll as I followed behind her. The formal dining room was always a sight to see. It was a long table, big enough for twenty people to sit at. It was often full for holiday parties that my parents would throw in extravagant fashion when we were growing up. It was always a big deal and the food was disgustingly fancy.

The type of food that a normal person would never eat.

I used to have to force it down, but

Danny was never able to. It got to the point that my parents would have Danny up in his room for the parties and just make up some lie about why he couldn't be there. I used to sneak him up real food, normally a cheeseburger from some fast food joint.

One of the antichrists according to my parents.

Fast food and junk food was never supposed to be in the house. We were to have healthy food and only healthy food. Some kids would hide porno magazines under their bed.

We hid chocolate bars.

Of course, my father sat at the head of the table with my mother sitting next to him. I had no choice but to sit on the other side. The food was, thankfully, not that bad. It was chicken and vegetables, at least.

"Good evening, father," I said as I sat down.

"You're late. A man of faith is never late."

"I'm sorry, father. Work ran late."

There was no point in telling him that a man of faith didn't kick his son out or disown him, either. Just like there was no point in telling him I hadn't stepped foot inside of a church since I left home on my eighteenth birthday last year.

He led saying grace before we were able to grab some of the food. I took a small portion because I knew my mother could barely cook. It might look good, but taste was a whole other beast.

"We need to talk about Daniel," my father started.

Apparently, we couldn't have a meal

together as a family without some ulterior motive. I had suspected something was going on when my father had called and ordered me to come for dinner tonight. Normally, when they reached out to me it was over the phone and it was to tell me about some event that I was apparently obligated to attend. I never did, but they still felt the need to reach out to me and tell me. They felt like they could control me, still, and I was not about to let them feel that way. Whenever I could avoid it, I always did. Tonight, I knew something was going on because they had never invited me over for a family meal.

We didn't do family meals.

We did fake shows for the society they were connected to. If my parents wanted to sit down and share a meal with just me, they wanted something and I'd suspected it had to do with Danny.

"He's doing great. He's getting all A's in school," I said. I knew that wasn't what they wanted to talk about, but I was not about to just yield to what they wanted.

"Lord knows what he's doing for those A's," my mother said under her breath, and I was instantly pissed off.

Of course she would think that Danny was trading in deviant sexual favors in exchange for a better grade. It wasn't even the fact that she thought Danny would have to stoop that low, but that she thought he couldn't be smart enough to get straight A's without the help.

Not to mention, what kind of teachers

did she think were at that school?

"We have tolerated this silly phase of his long enough. It's time to get serious. He needs to understand and see the light. He is not a queer. He is not a deviant living in sin. He needs to be cleansed of the demon inside of him and shown the light," my father lectured.

I was really getting sick of these beliefs of his. Homosexuality was only proof that demonic possession was real to him. It didn't matter how much scientific fact you provided him that sexual orientation was decided long before you were born. That it was within your genetic makeup and not some curse from God or the Devil trying to overtake your body.

"It's genetic, father. He can't control being gay any more than you can control being straight."

"Deviant behaviors can be controlled and corrected. I have reached out to a man that runs a facility that is equipped to handle this very situation. He runs a highly successful conversion camp and he has a place for Daniel."

A cold dread flooded my body.

He wanted to have my kid brother sent to a conversion camp?

Hell no.

I had heard of those places. It wasn't like a bible study group. They used any means necessary to try and rewire a person's brain to believe they were straight. They were taught how to suppress a major part of who they were just so they could fit in with what society dictated for a man to be. Danny couldn't go to a place like that. I wasn't going to let that happen.

"You can't send him to a place like that. Father, do you know what things they do to the kids there?"

He couldn't actually be educated properly on this. There was no way he would be willing to risk sending his own son there. They used any type of methods to "save" the boys there. Including sleep deprivation, starvation, abuse, borderline torture, and more. There was a reason the camps had been getting shut down whenever one was discovered.

"I am well aware of what goes on in the facility. I've already toured it. Daniel will learn how to be a real man and to finally be rid of this ridiculous phase. He will return to be a man of God and live how our Father wanted him to. It is on you to ensure he is here Saturday morning and ready to go. He doesn't need a bag, they will provide the proper clothing."

He actually thought I would not only agree to this, but to gift wrap my baby brother for them. That I could somehow convince him it was a good idea. He was more insane than I thought. There was no way I was going to allow this to happen. I would to do whatever I had to to ensure Danny was safe.

I'd stupidly thought they would just leave us alone. Allow Danny to stay with me until he was eighteen and then he would be an adult so it wouldn't matter. Now, though, I could see our father was not about to let that happen. He was not going to risk someone finding out that he had a gay son.

RESCUE

It looked like I was going to have to do something I had hoped to avoid, but now it seemed like the only way to save Danny from that level of pain. I would have to file for custody of him and fight my parents in court for him.

This dinner looked like it would be the last supper for our family. Because coming morning, it was going to be a bloody fight. One I was hoping Danny and me would survive.

CHAPTER TWO

Jay

WINNING A CASE would always feel amazing, especially when it was a case like this. A lovely gay couple had been trying to adopt a baby and the adoption center, the only one in town, had refused to allow them to adopt a beautiful baby girl because they were gay.

I was able to not only get them their

baby girl, but the adoption center would have to pay them their court fees and compensation for the discrimination.

The adoption center was also going to be getting a new CEO and would need to have a whole new set of protocols for the prospective parents.

To think that two good men who wanted to do something good by adopting a baby were being denied just because they were gay. That is what was wrong with not only this town, but the world.

Who cared if it was two men or two women that wanted to adopt a child that didn't have parents to love them?

If they were good people and could afford to raise a child, then they should get to.

It was this reason why I decided to

come here after law school. I grew up here in the foster care system and I knew first hand how much it sucked for a child. Plus, I was a gay child in the foster care system. Things for me were really not good and they had messed me up for a long time. Thankfully, I was able to get an early acceptance and a full scholarship to a pre-law program in Baltimore. I left at seventeen and I have never regretted it for a single second.

When it was time for me to decide what law firm I wanted to work for, I already knew the answer. I was coming back here and opening my own law office. I was going to help the LGBTQ community and foster kids. I wasn't going to let them be abused and forgotten about like everyone in town seemed determined to let happen.

Being twenty-four and running my own law office was not easy at all. I had busted my ass off in law school, taking courses during the summer and two extra courses a semester just to be able to graduate early. I have been back in town for a year now, working hard on bettering it and helping as many kids as I can.

I often volunteer for different charity events and youth shelters. My time was very filled, but I was okay with that. The result, though, was a lack of a personal life. I often worked late at the office on a case or learning something new. I was always reading up on different cases and new laws to keep myself ready for anything. My work consumed me and I was just fine with that.

Whenever I needed to take the edge

off, I would meet up with a friend with benefits. If I didn't have one at the time, I would go and meet up with someone in the gay bar or gay club in the next town over. It was a simple life, but it was mine and I wouldn't change it for a single second.

The tinkle of the bell above my door broke the silence and I looked over to see who was coming in. The man that walked through my door was not who I expected but I was very happy that he did decide to walk through my office door.

He was about my height and he had a very nice muscular body. He had a five o'clock shadow and he clearly wasn't shaving every day like I had to.

A curse of coming and going into court all week.

He wore a t-shirt and blue jeans with biker type boots. He had black grease stains on his jeans and his shirt, and I could tell that his hands were a bit dirty on the outside. This man clearly worked with his hands, a mechanic, if I had to bet. He didn't look that old, though. Not old enough to need a family lawyer, at any rate. I know, I shouldn't judge or make assumptions. Things happen. People get their girlfriend pregnant when they are teenagers, that wasn't unheard of.

"Are you Jay Dawson?" he asked, snapping me out of my thoughts.

"I am," I said as I held my hand out to him.

"Thad Smythe," he said as he took my hand.

The second our skin touched two

things happened. First, I could feel the calluses on his hand from being used for long hours, something that turned me on. Second, the fire that erupted from my chest at just this simple touch threw me for a loop. Leave it to my body to be attracted to the straight man.

"It's nice to meet you, Mr. Smythe. What can I do for you today?" I asked as I pulled back. This man was here for me to help him with some type of family law matter. I needed to stay professional.

"Call me Thad, and I was hoping you were able to take on a case right now."

"Of course. Please have a seat," I said as I gestured to the chairs in front of my desk.

I rounded my desk and took my seat as he sat down, his hands clasped in his lap. I could tell he was nervous and uncertain about being here. He wasn't the first client of mine that wasn't sure a family lawyer was a good idea. Having to go through the courts for custody of a child was never easy and it often was treated as a last resort. The majority of parents wanted to try and come to some sort of an agreement for the good of their child without having to drag the family through court.

"Can you tell me a bit about your situation, please?" I started.

"Um... yeah. My parents kicked my brother out about eight months ago when he came out to them. Danny, my brother, he's been living with me since then, and now my parents want to place him in a conversion therapy camp. Do you know what that is?"

A cold dread flooded my body. Oh, I

knew what it was all right. One of my foster parents had sent me to one when they discovered I was gay. I spent six months in that hellhole until I was able to convince them that I was cured.

What happened to me in that place was the whole reason I started getting involved in drugs and promiscuous sex. Those camps were designed to destroy young men and it almost won against me. My only saving grace was an old law professor who helped get me back on the right path when I was twenty-one. That was three years ago, and every year I send him a bottle of bourbon as a token of my thanks.

"I do, yes. How old is your brother?"

"He's sixteen, now. He's been living with me since he was fifteen."

"Okay, and have you spoken to your

parents about the conversion camp?"

"Last night, my father told me about it. They haven't spoken with Danny since they kicked him out. They are extremely religious and they refuse to have a gay son. He wanted me to bring Danny to the house so he could be taken. I told him what goes on in those camps and he said he didn't care. That he had already done a guided tour through one."

So, he was serious, then. That wasn't good, but it was grounds within court to get him away from his parents. I just needed to know what he was hoping for.

"Are you looking to have your brother in foster care or with you?"

"I want full custody of him. I'm nineteen, but I work full-time as a mechanic in town. I have a two bedroom apartment and he's been with me, like I said, for eight months. I've been taking care of him his whole life, practically. I even have some money saved up for his college education. I just need to keep him safe for two years and then our father can't do anything to him."

Jesus, he was only nineteen. He seemed older than that. That's a lot of responsibility for a nineteen year old. I had to give him credit, though, not every sibling would take their younger brother in and raise him. He was a good man and I was determined to help him. With his brother being sixteen, it might not be that difficult to win in court. He was practically an adult. It wasn't like he was a young child that required a great deal of care.

"Going for full custody is completely

possible. You have his age going in your favor. Because he's sixteen, he is able to make an intelligent decision as to where he would like to live. The judge will ask him if he would like to live with you or your parents, usually alone in his or her chambers. Due to you fighting against your parents, though, we will need to contact social services and have a case worker assigned to your brother."

"He'll have to be in foster care?" he asked with worry and fear flooding his voice.

"No, no, he can live with you. It's just the process because you are fighting both of your parents for him. A social worker will be assigned to Danny to ensure he is placed in the best possible home. They are there to fight for his rights, and based on what you said, they will fight to have him with you. They don't want kids being placed in those camps, either. They will offer whatever support they can to you and your brother. It's also another check mark in our favor in court."

He let out a sigh and I could tell he was still feeling a bit nervous about having a social worker around. Not that I could blame him. I knew that child protection services left a bad taste in a lot of people's mouth. They would be a good help in this case, though, and hopefully, after meeting with their worker, Thad would feel better.

"Okay, how do I go about filing?"

"I would draft the paperwork for you and then submit it to the court. It would then be served to your parents. They would hire a lawyer and draft their response, which we will get, as well. This happens pretty fast. Typically, within seven to ten days, we'll have the first court hearing. However, it could be up to a year before we have an official ruling. In the meantime, we will have to go back and forth to court. You won't need to be there for every hearing, just the really important ones. The first one isn't a big deal, it's always a continuance, but it has to happen."

"What's your hourly fee?"

"It's a hundred an hour."

It wasn't. It was actually three hundred an hour, but he seemed like he could use the break. I often would charge less if it was a special circumstance. This was one of those circumstances. I was not about to let Danny be trapped in a conversion camp.

Thad worked hard. I could see the exhaustion in his eyes. He was doing everything he could to provide for his brother. He didn't need to be left broke by the end of this.

"I'm assuming there's a contract I need to sign."

"Yes, it's pretty standard," I said, as I pulled it out.

I walked him through the whole contract and answered any of the questions that he had. By the end of it, I had a new client and he had some hope that his brother would be saved from his parents. This case was pretty straightforward and, with any luck, I would be able to get it solved with mediation.

And, hey, maybe by the end of it I would have a new friend in Thad, because he seemed like a man I wanted to have in my life.

CHAPTER THREE

Thad

I WAS EXHAUSTED, just completely exhausted and it was only the first week. For the past week, I had been working more hours than ever. I was up to about a hundred and twenty for this week. Thankfully, I got paid based on the jobs I did during the week. The more cars I fixed, the more money not only I made, but my boss made, too.

My boss was the only one happy about the amount of work that I'd been doing. I knew I couldn't keep this up for very long, but I had to push through for as long as I could. The small amount of money that I had saved up was for Danny's education and I didn't want it to disappear because I had to fight in court for custody of him. I had hoped that my parents would just let Danny go and for this whole thing to all be over and done quietly, but they weren't about to do that.

I truly thought they would. It wouldn't be public knowledge if it could be kept quiet and outside of a courtroom. It seemed like the perfect opportunity for them, yet they were fighting me on it.

RESCUE

We have our first appearance in two days and I knew I couldn't keep this quiet from Danny any longer. He was going to start to notice what was going on. People were going to talk and whisper in town. He didn't deserve to hear about it that way.

The only shining light in all of this was the fact that I had a lawyer who understood my position. Jay, he didn't have the most experience in town, but he was gay himself and an active supporter within the small LGBTQ community in town. He would understand how dangerous a conversion camp was and he would fight with me to keep Danny from ever having to step foot into one.

What was not helping me was the fact that Jay was sexy as hell, even for a guy that wears a suit all the time. I couldn't say I had a type, because up until six weeks ago I thought my type was a woman. I had noticed that some guys in town were good looking, but I had never felt a strong attraction to them, not like I felt with Jay.

The second his hand touched mine it sent electricity all up my arm and then right down to my crotch. He had soft features and he was clean shaven. He was also built, like a man that enjoyed working out but didn't spend all day at the gym. He wasn't massive, just a nice size. Model size, I guess you could call it.

I was built, too, but my muscles came from lifting heavy machinery and car parts. I didn't go to the gym, with my job I didn't have to. We were even the same height. But again my nervousness and confusion started to kick in because my mind automatically went to random questions.

Like, who would bottom?

It might seem like a stupid point to get stuck on, but I couldn't help it. I really didn't know what way I went and it really wasn't helping that when I thought about either position, neither of them bothered me. It wasn't like I had this knee jerk reaction to one over the other. They both left me feeling the same. It was a mess, but it wasn't a mess I needed to get sorted tonight or in the near future. I was too busy working to even have time for a dating life.

Tonight, was the night I was not looking forward to. It wasn't because I was worried Danny wouldn't handle the news very well. He would be okay with me getting sole custody of him. It was the fact that our own parents wanted to send him away to be abused at a conversion camp. Not to mention the reality that if I didn't get custody of him, that place would be his hell for the next two years. He would be stuck there until he either turned eighteen and could legally sign himself out, or our parents' grew a heart and let him leave. The second option was never going to happen.

It wasn't fair to put him in this position, but I didn't have a choice. I had to tell him, just like I had to fight in court for him.

Walking into the apartment, I instantly noticed the smell of spaghetti. God, I love my brother. He had been really good with me working so many hours, even before this past week.

That was one of the main issues I was worried about. If my parents' lawyer wanted to, they would easily be able to find out just how many hours I was working and how many hours Danny was home alone. Now, he was sixteen, but that could still be used against me. It was a total mess right now and all I could do was hope that it worked out.

It was just after nine at night and Danny was chilling on the couch watching something on the television.

"Hey little man, how was school?" I asked, as I headed into the kitchen to grab a soda. I needed to eat, but I wanted to talk to him first.

"It was great. School's out for the summer, now, and I don't have to deal with any of the idiots there."

My brother was not in the popular category at school. He was one of less than four gay kids in the whole school and it didn't really make him popular. Add in the fact that he was a complete nerd, chess team included, and he was not winning any points with bullies. The break for two months was going to do wonders for him.

"It'll be nice for you to have the break. Have you thought about what you want to do this summer?" I asked, as I sat down in the chair by the couch.

He had been thinking about working, but he wasn't sure where. I wasn't pushing it, because I wanted him to be able to be a kid and not have to stress about money. I wanted him to focus on his school work and not have to try and balance it all, like I did. I knew working would allow him to learn responsibilities and the value of money, but he already knew all of that.

He balances my check book.

"I was thinking about volunteering at a few different businesses to get my community service hours done. I also thought it would help me to figure out what I want to do after high school."

That was going to be his issue. He was so smart, but he had no idea what he wanted to do with it. He knew he wanted to go to College, but he had zero clue as to a program, yet.

"I think that's a really great idea. It'll let you get a feel for different jobs and see which ones you like and which ones you hate."

He flicked the television off and turned to face me before he spoke. "Are you sure, though, you don't want me to work? I can work during the summer and help out around here."

"I told you, your only job is to be a kid. I want you to focus on living your life and figuring out what you want when high school is over. That's the most important thing you have to worry about. It's my job to worry about the bills and it's your job to be a kid."

I didn't really get to be a kid when I was his age. I was too busy working my ass off so I could graduate high school and get my own place. I was too busy with my escape plan.

Danny didn't have to worry about that and I didn't want him to go through what I did. He deserved to be just a kid and I was going to work my ass off to ensure he got the next two years to do just that.

"I know, but I can help."

"I know you can and I appreciate the offer. You want to help out, make sure your laundry is done, and I would not say no to more of your cooking," I said, flashing him a warm smile.

"Deal," he said, giving me an easy smile back. I hated that I was going to have to be the one to remove it within the next three seconds.

"There is something we need to talk about, though," I started.

"What's going on?"

There was no easy way to tell him this, so I wasn't going to make it worse by tiptoeing around the conversation. "Last week, our parents wanted me to go over for a family dinner. I knew they had to be up to something, that's why I didn't bring you."

"We don't do family dinners, so what did they want?" he asked, already on edge.

"Father wanted me to help him with getting you to a conversion therapy camp."

"Conversion therapy? He actually wants to send me away to one?" He was angry now, but I also knew later on the betrayal and hurt would kick in.

"You know how religious they are, and you know how they feel about homosexuals. I thought he would leave you alone, that he would accept that you were living with me and be done with it. Apparently, that assumption was wrong. He wants to end this *phase*, as he called it, and get you back to being the way God designed you to be."

"That's bullshit. Even if you wanted to argue that God made me with a specific design in mind, I was born gay. You could argue that this is exactly how God wanted me to be."

Neither one of us was religious, but we could argue against it anytime we needed. We had gotten very good at flipping the tables on people. The problem was, when it came to heavily devoted religious people, it didn't matter what you said they were always going to believe they were right.

"I know. I told him that it's genetic and you were born attracted to men just like he was attracted to females. He wasn't going for it. He thought that I would help him get you there. I told him I was not going to be doing anything to help him and I would make sure to stop him from getting to you."

"But until I'm eighteen they have custody of me. I'll have no choice if they come here to grab me." The worry was now starting to kick in and I knew it was going to get worse before it got better.

"I know, and that is why I went and hired a lawyer. I'm suing them for full custody of you."

The shock was instant and it spread all across his face. I knew it wasn't something he ever thought would happen. This was never even a conversation we'd had. Neither of us ever thought we would need to fight for custody of him. We'd both believed that our parents would allow him to live here for the next two years without a problem. They didn't want to be a part of gossip or have their dirty laundry blowing in the wind. It made the most sense for them to keep it all quiet and not want a court hearing.

"Wait, what?" he asked, trying to get his mind to work.

"I know this is a shock, but it's the only way I can guarantee that you will never have to step one foot inside of a conversion camp. It's the only way I can protect you from him."

"Will they let you?"

"Our parents, no they are fighting against it, but while the court hearing is going on you will stay with me. As for the court, I honestly don't know if I'll win. I promise you, though, I will do everything within my power to win. To keep you here with me, where you are safe and can be free to be yourself. My lawyer, *our* lawyer, said there's a good chance that you could stay here. That with you being sixteen you can testify and tell the judge who you want to live with. He might be able to get this resolved quickly so you can move on with your life and they can leave you alone."

I was really hoping Jay would be able to pull this off. The last thing I wanted to do was to have to tell my kid brother that I had failed him. That I couldn't protect him from our parents.

"Okay, okay. What... what do I do?"

He was trying to wrap his head around this information and I was incredibly proud of him. He was trying to be strong and supportive and helpful. It was exactly the type of man he was and I loved him for it.

"All I need you to do is to be yourself. Is to go and hang out with friends and have a great summer. That's all you have to do. I will worry about the court stuff. I'm the adult and you are the kid, that was the deal we made when you moved in here eight months ago. Nothing changes that."

He didn't need to worry about this. He didn't need the added stress. He deserved to have a normal teenage life and I was going to make sure he had it.

"That's not fair to you."

"Life isn't fair, but I can handle it, little man. You be sixteen and I'll be the adult. That's the best way you can help me. I promise, I'll be okay and everything will be okay."

I didn't care how many hours I would have to work. I didn't care if all we ate was bologna sandwiches. I was going to make sure he stayed right here with me.

This was his home and there was no way in hell was I ever going to let anyone, especially my parents, take him from me.

CHAPTER FOUR

Jay

THIS WAS NOT my first court hearing, but for some reason I was more nervous today than I was on my first court hearing. I had done this plenty of times, helped children to be safe and be placed within the right home. To make sure that bad parents didn't get to keep abusing their children. This was not new to me at all. I had dealt with quite a number of cases just like this.

Yet, it wasn't exactly the same. I had never had a child's literal life in my hands. If I wasn't able to get Thad custody of Danny, there was a huge likelihood that Danny would be trapped in a conversion therapy camp for the next two years.

I didn't want that for him.

I didn't want that for anyone.

I wouldn't wish it on my biggest enemy.

It was hell in those camps and I knew guys often didn't make it out alive. The ones that did were so messed up they were never able to live a normal and healthy life again. Danny's case wasn't just if he should live with his mother or father, it was if he would have any chance of living a normal and healthy life. There was a great deal of pressure on this case and I really couldn't afford to lose it.

At the sound of footsteps coming down the hallway, I turned to see who it was. I had gotten to know quite a few of the people that worked here and I often said hello as they walked by. Sometimes, they would stop for a quick chat.

I was surprised to see Thad coming toward me. What was more surprising was what he was wearing. When he came into the office he was wearing his work clothes. He'd had grease on his pants and his shirt, his hands were slightly dirty with grease that had stained them. He was a working man, something I found very sexy.

Today, though, it was as if he had an

identical twin, but one that worked in the corporate world. He was wearing a suit. A very nice black suit. His hair wasn't messy from his fingers being run through it all day. He was clean shaven and no evidence of a five o'clock shadow existed on his face. He looked like he could be a lawyer himself.

The vast contrast between the two appearances had me dizzy. He looked just as sexy in a suit as he did in grease-stained clothes.

How the hell was that even possible?

"Good morning," I said as Thad reached me.

"Morning," he said as he fiddled with his jacket sleeve.

He looked the part, but he was nowhere near confident enough for the part. He was nervous and worried, not that I could blame him. I was nervous for Danny's sake and he wasn't my brother. I couldn't imagine how Thad was feeling right now. He was doing the right thing by taking his brother in and trying to keep him safe. Trying to allow him to be a kid and discover who he was. He was a good man, but that didn't mean that he was going to be able to handle this case.

"You don't have anything to worry about. Nothing is going to happen today. It's the first hearing, so all either side is going to do is ask for more time. They need more time, just like we do, to prepare their case. That's why I said you didn't have to worry about being here."

Nothing ever happens at the very first court hearing. Especially, when it came to custody cases. The majority of the court hearings would be continuations until both sides are ready. Then, we'd have to go through mediation to see if the issue can be resolved outside of a judge's ruling. If not, then we'd present our case to the judge and he or she decides where the child will go. We would also need to meet with Danny's new social worker to see what he or she would like from Thad and try to get them on our side. If we could get the social worker to side with us, that would cement us in the win category. Judges in family court always go with whomever the social worker is backing.

"I know, but I wanted to show that I was serious about this. I don't want to miss any of the hearings, even if they are going to be postponed. This is my kid brother's life on the line. It's worth the time to stand around in a courthouse, even if nothing happens."

This was serious to him. Very serious. I had plenty of clients that didn't show for court hearings until they were told they needed to be here. I'd never had any client show up for the first one. He wanted to make a good impression, even if it wouldn't be remembered. To him, it was worth the hassle of getting a suit on and standing around waiting for our turn. He was a good man and that made him even sexier.

I reached out and placed my hand on his bicep, his firm and muscular bicep. The second my hand made contact with him, electricity started to work it's way up my arm and into my stomach. It was insane, because all I did was touch his bicep, a bicep that was covered by material. It wasn't even like it was skin on skin. If it felt this good to touch him against clothes, I couldn't even imagine how it would feel to be skin on skin.

It would never happen. I couldn't let it happen. To begin with, I didn't even know if he was gay, that was for starters. Second, he was my client and I was not about to get a reputation for sleeping with my clients. I needed to be professional, regardless of how attractive he was. Nothing would ever happen between us so my body would just need to calm down and accept that.

"It's sweet that you want to be here. I know this is hard and nerve wracking, but it'll be okay. I promise, no matter what happens, I will not rest until we are able to get Danny with you."

I shouldn't be promising that, but I was feeling good about this. All the judge would need to hear is that they wanted to place him within a conversion camp and the judge would rule in Thad's favor. We would need to find proof, but that could happen during discovery.

I would be petitioning the courts for access to phone records, emails, and bank account statements to try and find irrefutable proof that his parents were looking to place Danny in one of those camps.

He was also sixteen and able to speak up for himself and state who he would prefer to live with. With him living with Thad for the past eight months after he was kicked out for being gay, it should be a straight open and shut case.

"Sorry, I'm not good with this type of

stuff. Give me a machine and I can take it apart and fix it. But stick me in a room with fancy dressed people using very big words and I'm reaching for a dunce cap."

He said it lightheartedly, but I could tell he was feeling self-conscious and insecure. Court had a way of turning even the most confident of men into timid little boys.

I could tell by our limited number of conversations that he was smart, but his mind was built to be able to handle mechanics. I believed him when he said he could fix any machine. Being in a courtroom, though, wasn't as simple as taking apart a machine. Not that I would consider that simple, but the principal behind it was. Take piece after piece off until you find the problem.

Courtrooms, though, the law, it was a

sequence of twists and turns and often you found a dead end. It was like trying to navigate through a maze in the pitch dark and you don't have anything but a small glow stick to get you through.

"The law isn't simple, it's very complicated. It's a lot of hard work in law school for seven years to even begin to understand half of what it is. You have no reason to feel like an idiot, because you're not one. The fact that you are here says everything that you need to say."

I didn't want him feeling stupid or insignificant. He was a good brother, I knew that when he told me he was working over a hundred hours just to provide a home for his brother and to save up for a college fund. He was doing everything he could for him. He was a good man and he did not deserve to feel like a moron. Before any more could be said, the voice over the speaker called our names and it was time for us to go inside.

"All you have to do is sit beside me up front. I will do all of the talking, which will be very little. We're just going to ask for more time, just like them," I reminded him.

He gave a nod and we were moving to head inside. The room was empty with the exception of the court clerk and the bailiff that stayed in the room. We got on our side and just as we sat down the door opened and his parents' lawyer came in.

Fuck.

They'd hired Ken Arnold.

He was a family lawyer from

Baltimore and he was a fucking shark. He owned a huge law firm with thirty lawyers underneath him. He had zero morals. He had no problem lying, stealing, cheating, doing whatever it took to win. And he always made sure to win, because his clients were paying him a thousand dollars an hour. Plus, he got a bonus of thirty thousand dollars if he was able to win your case within a set time.

He wasn't going to delay. He was going to push to get this case in front of the ruling judge as soon as possible.

I had never gone up against him because no one in town that had the money to afford him had children that wanted to leave. Thad's parents were far wealthier than I thought. They would also be paying him to keep this as quiet as possible. There would be gag orders coming our way. I was certain of that.

The judge walked in and I stood, making sure Thad did as well. Once the judge was sitting, I instructed Thad that he could sit down.

"Good morning, gentleman. Let's make this quick. This is your first hearing in regards to Smythe verses Smythe. I am assuming you both would like a continuance," Judge Wilson started.

"Yes, your Honor," I stated.

"No, your Honor. My clients would like to have this resolved as quickly as possible. We are going to push for a quickened process. I'd like to schedule the final hearing for two months from now," Ken started.

I could see Thad tense up beside me.

He had no idea who Ken was, and I would have to tell him about it afterward.

"Your Honor, this case is not straight forward. We need time to gather the proper evidence to prove that Mr. Arnold's clients are looking to place my client's sixteen year old brother into a conversion therapy camp for being gay. This case is very serious and should not be rushed and handled with a messy due process."

"Allegations, your honor. There's no proof of anything that Mr. Dawson is laying claim to," Ken argued immediately.

"Mr. Smythe told my client over dinner that he wanted my client to ensure that his brother was brought to the house so he could be driven to the camp. Mr. Smythe stated that he had already spoken with the camp organizer and had seen it already. We are talking about the mental and physical welfare of a sixteen year old boy. The only reason Mr. Arnold wants a speedy process, is because of the bonus he receives to get a case resolved before a set date. That date is sixty days, your Honor. Mr. and Mrs. Smythe are very religious people, as I am sure you know, your Honor. You know how they would react to having a gay son."

"If you know my clients personally, your Honor then I am requesting to have a new judge assigned to this case. One that does not have a personal connection to either family," Ken immediately tossed out.

Judge Wilson held his hand up to

stop the both of us. He was not prepared for any of this, that much was clear. "Mr. Arnold, you are not from here so allow me to explain how things work in my town. First, everyone knows everyone so you won't find a judge in this town that doesn't know the Smythe's. Second, you might be used to doing things fast in the big city, but in this town, in this courthouse, we make sure that every child is safe regardless of age. If any of the accusations are true in regard to your client's wishes with the child in question, then this court will make sure the child is safe. And Mr. Dawson, I do not take lightly the accusations of a conversion camp being thrown around so, for your sake, I hope you can back them up with solid evidence. We are going to reschedule this case for thirty days from now where I will determine if there is more to the accusations or if we move on to mediation. Thirty days, gentlemen," Judge Wilson said as he banged his gavel, and I knew he was done.

Before Thad could say anything, I turned to him and held my finger up to my lips to ensure he wouldn't say anything. We were not going to be talking where Ken could overhear us. Just like we were not going to be talking to him. I grabbed my briefcase and Thad followed me out of the courtroom. I waited until we were outside before I got into my car and gave a nod to him to do the same. Once we were safely in my car, Thad spoke.

"What was that?"

"Ken Arnold, he owns a family law

firm in Baltimore with thirty lawyers underneath him. Ken is a thousand dollar an hour lawyer who will receive thirty grand if he wins your case within sixty days. He's a shark and he holds zero morals. He will lie, cheat, and steal, if that means he will win. He will intimidate witnesses and badger the children in question to get them to drop it and pick his client to live with."

"That's great, just fucking great," he said as he rubbed his hands over his face.

He was getting stressed, not that I could blame him. But Ken was my problem and not his. I would have to be the one to deal with him and I was not going to roll over for him. I didn't care how much experience he had, he was not going to win.

"We have a huge benefit in our corner. We're not in Baltimore. Smaller towns have a way of doing things and he's not going to be very good at playing by our rules. We also have things going for us. We have a social worker that will be getting involved and meeting with you and Danny. They are on Danny's side and only want what is best for him. Danny is also old enough to testify and say where he wants to stay. And if nothing else, and the worst should happen and we lose, he's sixteen. He can turn right around the very same day and file for emancipation."

That was my hail Mary, but it was a card we could play should the worst happen and I lose this case. He was sixteen and there was no reason why he couldn't file for it.

"What is that?"

"An emancipation allows the child to petition the court for them to be legally an adult. If he was granted the emancipation, he would no longer be under your parents' care. He would be considered an adult in the eyes of the law. So he could open his own bank account, get an apartment, everything a normal eighteen year old would be able to do. Once the paperwork is filed, he can live on his own and there is nothing your parents could do until a ruling was decided."

"So we have a back up plan?" Thad asked, looking for confirmation.

"Yes. I don't like doing it, if I can help it. It would be better for him if he could be placed in your custody, but if shit hits the fan, we can go down that route.

Even if he doesn't get the emancipation, I can petition the court for a review. We can keep filing for reviews and continuances to try and delay it by two years. We only need to get him to eighteen and I can do that by filing different court cases to keep him away from your parents."

"Like a very expensive version of keep away."

It would be expensive and time consuming, but I didn't want him to worry about that right now. He had enough he needed to worry over.

"Basically, but we only need to get him two years. We can do that."

"As long as he never has to step foot into a conversion camp, it'll be worth it," he said with complete honesty.

"Let's focus on this current case. I'll

work on gathering proof of what your parents' intentions are with Danny. You worry about taking care of him. I will let you know when the social worker reaches out to me. He or she will want to check out your apartment and speak with you both."

He gave a nod before he spoke. "I appreciate it."

He got out of my car and I couldn't help but notice the loss of his presence. I needed to stop thinking about him like that. He probably wasn't even gay to begin with and he was my client. I needed to focus all of my energy and effort on finding proof and saving Danny from a horrific pain. I was taking Ken Arnold down and I was going to ensure that Thad and Danny ended up together where they belonged.

CHAPTER FIVE

Thad

THE MUSIC WAS obnoxiously loud tonight, but that was to be expected when you were in a club. It wasn't often I went to a bar or a club, but tonight I just needed a bit of an escape. Some time to unwind after working so much.

Danny was off at Jimmy's for the night, giving me the opportunity to relax and be nineteen. I had gotten a fake ID when I was eighteen, but I hadn't used it very often. This was only the third time I'd been to a bar or a club, and it'd always been a gay club or bar. Each time I came here, it'd been with the courage to finally do something. To finally dance with another man or kiss one, but each time all I did is sit there in a booth looking out at the crowd as I nursed a beer. I wanted to be out there with the other guys. I wanted to be brave and confident, like they all seemed to be, but I wasn't. I didn't know how to do this. I didn't know how to flirt or interact with someone I found attractive. Growing up had failed me in that department.

"Thad, hey."

I looked up from my beer bottle to see Jay standing in front of me. Seeing him sent an electric shock throughout my body. Gone was the stuffy suit and in its place was black jeans, black t-shirt, and a black leather jacket. He looked good.

Very good.

Deliciously good.

And that was not helping my growing attraction to him.

It had been a week since our court hearing and I hadn't seen him since. I had an appointment with a social worker in two days. He was coming by the apartment and tomorrow I would be spending my time outside of work cleaning the whole place up. I knew Jay was gay, but for some reason I never thought he would be here. That our paths would ever cross outside of our working relationship.

"Jay, how are you?"

I hadn't told anyone that I was gay, not even Danny. But here I was sitting in a gay club, so obviously I was gay or bi-sexual, but saying it seemed so official, and I'm not sure I was ready for people in my life to know. Not that I had many people in my life. Outside of Danny, I only had a couple of friends from the garage, certainly not enough to throw a coming out party.

"I'm good. I would ask where you got the fake ID, but you probably got it from the same person I did when I was younger," he said, following with a chuckle as he sat down in the booth with me.

"I don't use it very often," I said, trying not to sound awkward.

"You work a lot. I'd imagine you don't have much time for anything but work and sleep."

Another reason why I haven't dated anyone, because I don't have much time for anything outside of working and sleeping. Yes, I could make the effort to find the time with the right person, but I haven't found the right person to make it work. It also didn't seem fair to the other person to not have the time for them.

"My parents keep calling. I don't answer, but they call me ten to fifteen times a day." I switched topics to something that was more comfortable to me.

"That's normal at the start of a case. Don't answer the calls and save the voicemails so we can use them later, if we need to. If it goes on for much longer, I can petition the court to have a no contact order placed against them. They seem like control freaks."

Understatement of the year. Especially where my father was concerned. He had to make sure you did everything he wanted, just the way he wanted it.

"Everything always had to be perfect. The house had to be perfect. We had to look perfect. We had to be perfect, perfect behavior, perfect grades, just perfect."

"I'm sorry, that couldn't have been easy. It makes for a very stressful and anxious life," he said with a gentle voice.

"Got through it. I protected Danny from it, as much as I could. Covered for him when something wasn't done just right. Made sure he got to go out and hang with his friends."

"So, you guys have always been

close?”

“Had to be. Loving and caring are not personality traits that my parents have. When one was sick, the other was there. When we needed to talk or cry, the other was there. We told each other everything. We had no secrets. And now, I'm hiding something from him,” I said, letting out a sigh as I sat back against the booth.

“He doesn't know you are gay,” Jay easily stated.

“Nope. I know he won't care. Telling him wouldn't be a big deal to him.”

“But it would be for you. You're new,” he said with complete understanding.

Painfully new.

I didn't have any interest in talking about this, but at the same time he was gay himself. He seemed like the nonjudging type, especially with what he did for a living.

Maybe this was what I needed.

The chance to talk about what I had been worried about.

"Dating wasn't really allowed growing up. Whenever I was with a girl, I had to be supervised by my father. My parents are heavily religious and believe that your first kiss should be to your wife, standing in front of God at the altar. Growing up, I never kissed a girl. I had never really been attracted to one, but I hadn't looked at a guy that way, either."

"So what changed?" he asked, genuinely interested in hearing more.

"I don't know. I moved out on my eighteenth birthday, but even then I didn't date anyone. I was never attracted to anyone and I figured it was normal.

Even watching porn, it did nothing. Then one time, I picked a video clip with two guys and a girl and the two guys started to do things with each other. That was the first time I could honestly say I was aroused. It opened up some questions, but I haven't acted on it yet."

"How long has it been?"

"Six weeks."

"Shit, you are new." He paused for a moment before he continued and I knew what just clicked in his head. "Wait, if you've never kissed anyone before you were eighteen and you haven't been attracted to anyone since then, have you been kissed?"

I just simply shook my head no. There was nothing more to say to that, really.

"You're a gold star virgin. Shit, you're

a unicorn," he said, flashing a big smile.

"That's not exactly a good thing. It makes everything awkward and confusing."

"I can understand that. So, let's work it out. You must have questions. I probably have the answers. I've known I was gay since I was a kid."

"I don't know... You're my lawyer."

I didn't want to make things between us awkward. It was already going to be awkward now that he knew that I was gay and had never been kissed.

I was nineteen; it was basically unheard of.

Even Danny had been kissed.

My kid brother had more of a sex life than I did and that was pathetic and sad.

Jay wasn't someone that I would

never see again. I would have to see him outside and inside of court. It would be better to keep things professional with him.

"Which means you already know I can keep things confidential and a secret. Look, there's not much you could tell me that I already haven't heard. I've heard worse, a lot worse. You have questions, who else are you going to ask?"

No one.

That was the issue.

I had no one that I could ask. It wasn't like I could ask Danny. He wasn't old enough for that type of conversation. Plus, he didn't need to know about my lack of sex life. It was one thing for him to ask me, but not the other way around. And thankfully, he had quite a few gay friends and any questions he had he was asking them. I didn't have anyone that I could ask questions to. Maybe Jay wasn't that bad of an option, after all.

"I'm just... I'm not good at this type of thing. I don't know how to flirt. I don't know how to make that first step. I didn't get that in high school, and when I was on my own, I was working all the time to take care of Danny. I mean, say I do find a guy and we kiss and things are progressing, I don't know if I'm a top or a bottom. How do I even know that?"

He gave me a warm smile and ordered us two new drinks when the waitress walked by before he gave me his full attention.

"You are asking yourself all the right questions. Questions every single gay man has ever asked themselves. First, flirting is hard for a lot of guys. It's why it's best to just be yourself and not worry about trying to come up with some pick up line. Just be you and if the other guy is feeling it, you'll know. Second, some guys know they are a top, and some guys know they are a bottom. A lot of alpha males are tops, because to them being underneath another man is a turn off. Some guys love being on the bottom because it feels better to them. It's a personal choice. One only you can make."

"But how do I make that choice? What if I make the wrong one?"

I think that is what scared me the most. Being with a man and having my first time being terrible because it didn't feel good, because I topped when I should have bottomed, or vice versa. Your first time was supposed to be special and it was supposed to feel amazing and it wouldn't if I picked the wrong one.

"When you are in the moment, you'll know. I know, that is a shitty answer, but it's honest. When you are with a man and things are getting hot and heavy, your body will tell you that you either want to be inside of him or him inside of you. Your first time is a big one, it's supposed to be special and it's a lot of pressure you are putting on yourself by over thinking this. Let your body tell you and explore alone. If you are curious how it would feel like to have a man inside of you, then experiment with yourself. See if it feels good with your own hand, because if it doesn't, then chances are it won't with him. There's a reason sex toys exist," he said, flashing a big smile.

Instantly, I felt the heat creep up my neck and into my cheeks. The thought of walking into a sex shop was enough to make me blush, but to be talking about sex toys and me playing with myself. It was too much, way too much for me.

Jay let out a warm laugh as the waitress brought our drinks over and he paid for them.

"A blushing school boy," he teased before he continued. "You could be both, you know. I am."

"Both?" I asked, confused.

"Some guys are switches. It means we like to top and we like to bottom. Both feel good to us. You may find that you're a switch, too."

Huh, that was interesting.

I had never thought of that before. I always assumed it was one or the other. I had no idea which one I would prefer or if I would enjoy both, but that was interesting.

"And you said you're a switch?"

"I am. As long as it feels good, that's all that matters to me. Take the time to explore your own body and take your time with whoever you decide to be with. You have to be comfortable as you progress, otherwise it won't be enjoyable. And stop stressing over it. It will happen when it happens, and your body will let you know what it wants. God, you're nineteen. Have some fun, Thad."

Fun.

That was not a word I was used to. I didn't have time for fun. I knew at my age, most people were out having fun at parties and sleeping around. To me, I worked and that was pretty much it. I was okay with that. I didn't need to go out to parties and have a lot of friends. I was working, improving my skills and saving up money for Danny's education. That is what was important and what I focused on. Fun could always come later.

We spent the next few hours at the club hanging out and talking. We didn't talk about anything personal after that and we didn't talk about the case. Instead, I told him about different cars that I had been working on and he told me about some past cases. It was almost like we were friends and, for the first time since I had met him, I was hoping after the court case was closed that we could be friends. It would be nice to have another friend, especially one who was gay and knew I was gay.

We had both switched to water after a few beers, we were both driving, it was just after midnight when we headed out and he walked me to my car.

"That's a nice bike," I said with a nod to a beautiful motorcycle just a few cars away from mine.

"Thanks," he said with a grin.

"Wait, that's yours?"

Of course he had a motorcycle. The sexy, smart lawyer would obviously have a motorcycle.

Ugh.

As if he could get any hotter.

"It is. I've always wanted one growing up and I decided to get one after law school. A treat to myself for all of the hard work I went through to get my law degree."

"I don't blame you, it's one hell of an accomplishment. I bet you drive the guys crazy." I bit my bottom lip.

He was sex on a stick.

He probably had a phone full of numbers that he could call when he was in the mood.

"They do love it." He moved closer to me and placed his hand on my hip as he continued. "You know, we could make an agreement between us. You have no experience in the sex department and I have a lot. I could be your safe zone."

"Safe zone?" I managed to force out.

With him being this close to me, touching me even through clothes, it made it hard to think. It made it hard to form words. I had a feeling what he was getting at, but I needed him to say it.

"A person that you can experiment with. No strings attached, no pressure, just fun. You can share your firsts with someone that won't pressure you and can teach you all sorts of little tricks."

Oh, I bet he had tricks.

Damn.

I bet he could make me forget my own name.

He had a lot of confidence and the only time a man had this much confidence is from being very good.

But could I really cross that line with him?

Could he be my first?

I wasn't sure I wanted him to be the first man I slept with, but at the same time it's not like I had someone in mind. At the rate I was going, my first time was going to be with some stranger that I picked up in a club.

Why not let it be with someone that I sort of knew?

And we could go slow, build up to it. If nothing else, when I did find someone that wanted to date me, that I wanted to date, at least I wouldn't go into it as a gold star virgin. I would know how to do some things with him and not look like an idiot.

"Isn't it against the rules with me being your client?"

"Technically, your brother is my client with him being sixteen. We would just need to keep our professional and personal relationship separate. Church and state. What do you say?"

What do I say?

I knew what my body was screaming

at me to say. It wanted him. For the first real time in my life my body wanted another person. Being around him turned me on and it was a whole new feeling and experience for me.

Would it be smart to mess around with my lawyer?

No.

But if we kept it separate, if we didn't let it affect our professional relationship, then maybe it wouldn't be so bad. He didn't really come across as the type of guy that dated people. He worked long hours, I knew that much about him, so it wasn't like he had the time to date.

If it was no strings attached and just two guys having fun, could it really hurt?

I had spent my life being perfect. Being good enough for my parents, doing what they wanted me to do. I had spent my free time taking care of Danny from a very young age. I always put him first, put my responsibilities first. Maybe it was time I finally did something for myself. Maybe it was finally time for me to do something selfish.

"Kiss me."

A sexy smirk spread across his face. As he closed the distance between us, he moved his other hand up to cup the side of my face. He leaned in and his warm lips pressed against mine.

I tensed, slightly, as his lips touched mine, but he didn't pull away. He simply ran his thumb along my cheek to calm me down as he lightly kissed me. Once the initial shock wore off, I pressed my lips back against his and he started to truly kiss me.

I don't know what I was expecting it to feel like, but I knew nothing would have ever compared to this. There was no emotion or feeling that I could have possibly thought of that would ever have come close to what this felt like. My whole body was tingling, like I had been electrocuted and the effect was still lingering. The tingling started from my lips and worked its way all over my body and pooled in my crotch.

I felt his tongue swipe lightly against my lips and I wasn't sure what he wanted, but when he did it again, I opened my mouth slightly. It was as if my body just knew what to do, what he wanted and how to respond to him.

If I thought the feel of his lips against mine was erotic, it was nothing compared to the feel of his tongue lightly brushing against my own. A moan instantly escaped my mouth and it only fueled him on.

I allowed him to have control over the kiss. One, I was enjoying it, and two, I had no idea what I was doing and he clearly did. I melted into the kiss and allowed my body to enjoy the pleasure he was providing it.

When he pressed up against me, I could feel that he was enjoying this just as much as I was. At that moment, I would have loved to go further than just a kiss, but I was hyperaware that we were in a public parking lot and didn't need to give passersby a free show.

When the need for air became too great for the both of us, he pulled back, but placed one more gentle kiss to my lips before he pulled back and removed his hand from my face.

"When you're ready for the next lesson, text me."

He walked backward and gave me a wink before he turned and headed for his motorcycle. I had just barely managed to form a thought before he turned it on.

"Drive safe."

Not the most sexy thing to say, but it was all my brain could form. I stood there and watched as he pulled out and drove off into the distance. Even if I chickened out and never texted him after this, tonight was easily the best night of my entire life and that kiss would be haunting my dreams for months to come.

CHAPTER SIX

Jay

THIS CASE WAS going south a lot quicker than I thought it would be. I had wanted to get a warrant to search phone and email records for Danny's parents. However, *The Shark* was holding off on it. He was constantly throwing up that there was no probable cause for me to be interested in personal information. Also going as far as stating that Mr. Smythe uses both for his business and that would be breaching the confidentiality that his clients rely on.

Mr. Henry Smythe, owned a bank in town and my argument that he wouldn't have personal client information on his personal phone and email had been ignored. I needed to be able to prove that Mr. Smythe was looking to place Danny in a conversion camp. That was the only way this was going to go in our favor.

Today, I was meeting with Craig Brooks, the man that I suspected was running the conversion camp. I had done some digging and was able to find him as the only connection that other heavily religious parents had gone to for their troubled child. I had reached out to him as being a concerned brother.

I'd hoped to meet him at the camp, but he shot that straight down and said we were going to meet at a coffee shop. I hoped my sweet talk would be enough to get me an appointment at the camp, and then I could gather more information from him. If I couldn't get at Mr. Smythe's records, then I would have to get at Brooks and press him for the information.

As I walked into the coffee shop, Brooks was easy to spot. He was the only male sitting alone and he had two coffees there. I made my way over to him and he stood, holding his hand out as he spoke.

"Mr. Johnson?"

"Yes, it's a pleasure to meet you," I said, shaking his hand. I prayed he wouldn't recognize me. It was a small town, but we did have a decent number of people. I might not stand out if he hadn't been in court with me.

Brooks was a community counselor and his focus was on young teenage boys. He was looking for gay kids, to have parents pay him to keep them in his camp.

"It's nice to meet you. Please, have a seat. I got you a coffee," he said as he sat back down.

"Thank you. I truly appreciate you agreeing to meet with me. I am honestly at a loss of what to do with him," I said as I slid into the seat across from him.

"Why don't you tell me a bit about what is going on and I'll see what I can do to help."

"I grew up in the foster system and I met Chris in the system when he was only eight and I've been taking care of him ever since. He's fifteen, now, and he's been acting out."

I did grow up in the foster system and I did, at one point, have a kid brother named Chris that I took care of. He would have been twenty this year, if he had not been killed in the same conversion camp that I was sent to. He couldn't handle it anymore and he killed himself. He was only twelve and, to teach me a lesson, the camp leader made me dig his grave and bury him. The very next night, I escaped and made sure the place was shut down.

"Acting out, how?"

"He's angry, becoming violent, sneaking out and being out all night. I know he's been engaging in deviant sins with other men. I need it handled. I need him to go back to living a proper life, the life God would be proud of. I have heard whispers that you are the one to see. That you have a camp that can help put him back on the right path."

I had to be careful. I couldn't flat out ask him about his conversion camp, but I had to let him know that the camp was why I was talking to him and not some priest. It was a fine line and I wasn't even sure it would work. Guys like Craig Brooks didn't survive this long by being stupid.

"I offer counseling at a summer camp, though I don't think that will help him as it is for children with disabilities. I can put you in touch with a great priest who has performed many successful exorcisms to remove the demon within children. One even has a fiancé now," he said with a warm and proud smile.

He wasn't going to play ball with me. I hadn't earned his trust. He would only tell me about the camp if I jumped through all sorts of hoops, which I wasn't about to. Not only did I not have the time, but I was not about to put a child through any of those hoops. Still, I figured I'd try one more time before going to plan B, or plan C, I guess, at this point.

"Is there not a camp that I could send him to. A place that would help re-train his mind to think properly?"

"If you are suggesting, what I believe you are suggesting, those places are illegal and, as a man of God, I do not do anything illegal and I would advise you to follow the same path. The priest is very good and he will be able to help your brother. All you have to do is believe, my brother."

Fabulous, this man actually believes he's saving kids. There's no telling how many of those young gay boys he's sent off to his own camp to make money off of them. He might have won this round, but I was going to be winning the war with him. He would be in jail and his camp would be shut down for good.

***

A new day and a new plan.

I walked into the office of Alias Investigations to visit an old friend. And by friend, I mean, *with benefits*. Damien Anderson was a former something—he has yet to tell me what he did before he came into town. I suspected he was either in law enforcement, the military, or he was a gun for hire. I had no idea what one it was, but everything in me screamed it was the last one.

I knew nothing about him. For all I knew, his name was not Damien Anderson. I had no idea if he had family, where he was from, what he used to do, what his favorite color was even.

All I knew was that this man could go all night and never get tired. He had given me the best sex of my life, so far, and often when the itch came I would go to him. He also didn't date and I knew he preferred guys that could hold their own in a fight, but not be bigger than him. He didn't go for the spinner types.

The only reason I believed he was a gun for hire was based on the amount of tattoos he had and the number of guns. I had seen his long range sniper rifles on a couple of occasions and I'd noticed that the serial numbers were filed down. His bullets were also homemade, with his own machine, eliminating any paper trail of him purchasing a bullet that could tie back to him.

As a lawyer, it should bother me, but I was a family lawyer and as long as he wasn't aiming for me or a child, I was good with it.

He moved here five years ago and he opened up his own private detective firm. It was only him and another man who he claimed to be his best friend, though I suspected it was his brother. They looked way too much alike to just be friends. They had different last names and their own rundown version of a back story, but it never sat right with me.

The point, though, he was one hell of

an investigator and whenever I needed someone for a case to look into someone for me, I always went to him.

Today, I was going to see him about the conversion camp. I also wasn't going to be charging Thad for any of this. It wasn't just his fight anymore. I had to free those kids from that camp and make sure everyone involved paid the proper price, including the adults that sent the kids there.

I knew Damien would do this for free, anyway. He hated those camps just as badly as I did. Walking into his office, I noticed that no other client was there. Their office was not warm and welcoming, it wasn't designed for it. If you hired Damien, it was because you needed someone that wasn't afraid to break the law to get what you needed.

Normally, I wouldn't do that, but sometimes desperate measures were needed to keep a child safe.

Damien had no problem doing whatever it took to save the life of a child. It's why I always came to him. There was no judgment or lectures about morals and ethics. To him, it was straight forward. A child was at risk, so you did whatever it took.

"Long time no see, Sexy," Damien said as he sat back in his chair behind his desk. He could see me through his open office door as I wandered into the entryway. I headed over and closed the door once I walked in.

"It's good to see you, Damien. You're looking as good as ever."

"I'll be better tonight, if you swing by."

Tempting, very tempting, but I made a point in not sleeping with him when I needed his help. Plus, I had Thad on my mind and I was set to see him tonight. He had the social worker coming by his house first and then, I would see him.

"I got a job for you," I said as I slid into the chair in front of his desk with a shake of my head and a grin.

"Which means no sex. What is it?" he asked, with complete understanding in his voice.

"A client of mine is trying to get custody of his sixteen year old brother. Their parents are looking to send him away to a conversion camp that I believe is being run by Craig Brooks. He is a community counselor to teenage boys. I got his name through the grapevine of being the one to turn to when your gay son is becoming a problem and he needs to be reformed. I sat down with him yesterday at a coffee shop. He refused to meet anywhere else and played it off like he had no idea why his name would come up. He referred me to a priest who would perform an exorcism."

"And you like him for the camp?"

"I do. I can't legally run his finances, but as a counselor in that community building, I know he only makes just over forty grand a year. His house is over a million five. He just bought a boat, based on the social media pictures. He's getting the money from somewhere and he's not connected to a rich family. Him or his wife."

"And leaders of a conversion camp can make millions a year. How long do I have?"

"Two weeks, at most. The only thing keeping me alive in court is the claim of sending the kid to conversion therapy. His parents hired a shark, Ken Arnold, and he is pushing for this to end very quickly. I have until our next court hearing in two weeks to show proof that Mr. Smythe was in contact with the owner of the conversion camp. If not, I could lose this case."

He simply gave a nod. He knew how important this was and I knew he would find something for me, anything I could use to hold off on the case moving too quickly.

"Do you have any idea where it might be?"

That was the problem, it could be anywhere.

These camps were designed to be

kept hidden, to be kept under the radar. The owners were very good at making them appear as something else on the outside. It wasn't until you were inside did you know of the hell that was going on.

"I have no idea. And it's not like I can send my client in to speak with his parents and gather more info on it. They know he's not going to send his brother there."

"I'll handle it."

"Thanks. Just invoice me whatever the charge ends up being."

"Don't worry about it. This camp needs to be shut down. I ain't about to bill you for it. You know that."

I did know that, but I also didn't want to assume anything, either. We weren't in a relationship. We were barely friends with benefits. Truly, we were *fuck buddies*. If we were friends with benefits that would entail me knowing something about him that a friend would. All I knew is that if you pissed him off, you should run in zig zags, and he hated crimes against children. It wasn't much to go on, that was for sure.

"I didn't want to assume. You do a lot of hard work and I never want you to feel like I'm taking advantage of you."

"Appreciate it, but not necessary. Anything that goes against children is always something we will take on free of charge. You can pay me in sex when the case is done," he said, offering me a rare smile and a wink. It was weird because when he smiled, he looked even more dangerous.

"Looking forward to it," I said as I

stood up.

I knew he would want to get to work on it and I had my own digging to do. I needed to find something that I could use just in case Damien wasn't able to pull through for me on time. He would find the camp, I knew that without a doubt, but it just might not be in time for the next court appearance. If that happened, I would need something else that I could use to bide my time.

Danny had a lot of people in his corner and we were not going to give up, no matter what.

CHAPTER SEVEN

Thad

AT THE KNOCK at the door, I did one more quick visual sweep of the place to ensure everything was in proper order. I wasn't like my parents, I didn't need the place to be spotless, but when someone from Child Protective Services was coming by to see the home that I was providing for my brother, it needed to be spotless. That meant no dirty socks randomly on the floor, or a questionably clean floor and dirty dishes in the sink. It all needed to be perfect so he or she wouldn't think I couldn't handle caring for my brother.

A lot was riding on this and I was going to make sure there was no question on if I could take proper care of Danny. I had never gone through something like this before, so I wasn't sure what they were going to ask or what they wanted from me. For all I knew, I could already be behind in what they were hoping to see.

I had made sure to schedule for when Danny was out volunteering. They didn't say specifically that he needed to be here for this, so I was going to keep him away as long as possible. He didn't need to be wrapped up in all of this until it was absolutely necessary.

Letting out a slow, deep breath, I made my way toward the door and opened it for the social worker. There, on the other side of the door, was a man about my age. If I had to guess, I would say twenty-one, and he was thin. He weighed maybe a hundred and twenty pounds, if he was lucky. He had a young looking face, but he didn't look very mean. His eyes were warm and friendly so I was hoping he wouldn't drill into me about every tiny detail of our lives.

"Mr. Smythe?" he asked.

"Yes, call me Thad, please. Come in," I said as I moved back and allowed him to enter my apartment.

He walked in and I could instantly see his gaze flitting all over the place, scooping it out. I couldn't help but feel self-conscious about all of this. I had no idea what he would consider to be good enough and what would happen if I didn't meet his expectations.

"I'm Travis Manning and today, I just want to see where Danny is living and ask you a few questions," he said as he turned his attention to me.

"Of course. Please, have a seat. Can I get you something to drink?" I was really hoping my nervousness was not coming through. I didn't want him to think I had something to be nervous about.

"No. Thank you. I'm just going to look around, if that is all right?"

It wasn't like I was going to have much of a say in it. If I said no, that would make it look like I had something to hide. I simply gave a nod and stood there as Travis made his way down the hallway and poked his head into every room. He ignored my room, for the most part, and focused on the bathroom and Danny's room.

I had made sure Danny's room was cleaned up and there was nothing hidden away that Danny was trying to get by me. He was a really good kid, though, and I never had to worry about him sneaking alcohol or drugs into the house. Once Travis came back, we both sat down in the living room and I knew things would get started.

"I would like to start by saying, I am not here as an enemy to either you or Danny. I am here to ensure that Danny is in the best place possible. With him being sixteen, he may only have two years left, but those two years are still important. I will be speaking with Danny, as well, and see what he thinks and how he feels about living with you and your parents. I will take everything into consideration before I make my final decision on who would be best to be Danny's guardian. Do you have any questions for me?"

"Will you be coming by often?"

I knew I needed to ask something, but my mind couldn't seem to put words together just yet. I didn't want to seem like I didn't care by not asking something. I was hoping as this meeting progressed that I would be able to think of intelligent things to say.

"I will be coming by once a month until there has been a ruling. It is just to ensure that everything with Danny is going well and to be a support to the both of you. You are nineteen, you're still young, and I want to make sure you have all the support you need to be the best guardian for Danny," Travis said with a warm smile.

"Okay, we have nothing to hide, ask away," I said, hoping I sounded confident.

"How long have you been raising Danny?" he started.

"Alone, eight months, now, but before that it'd been me mostly raising him. I started to take over when I was eight."

"Where were your parents?" he asked, slightly confused.

I had never met him before, but if he lived in this town for more than a week, he would have heard about my parents. They were the church going socialites that stood out. Everyone knew them and everyone believed they were good people and amazing parents. It was always expected to keep that image going, it was why I was so surprised that they wanted to go through with this court case.

"My parents, they aren't loving or caring people. They put on a good show for the public, but behind closed doors, we were an inconvenience to them. Everything had to be perfect. The house, our appearance, our grades, everything always perfect. I got used to it easier than Danny. He had a harder time. He's really smart, but he's also sensitive. He needed a physical and an emotional connection to strive. My parents weren't interested in either, so I filled that void. I made sure he was taken care of. I potty trained him. I was there when he had a nightmare. I made sure he had food, got his homework done. When he was sick, I took time off from school to care for him. Whenever he got to go on a field trip that we knew my parents would never allow, I gave him the cash and forged their signatures. I covered for him when there was a mess in the house so he wouldn't be punished. I snuck food in for him when our parents had him hidden away in his room when their friends came over. I told him about sex and he came to me first when he discovered he was gay."

To some, I knew it sounded bad, but to me that was life. This was my life. I was the older brother and it was on me to take care of him. I didn't feel like I had been cheated out of a childhood or that he was a burden. He's my kid brother and there wasn't anything I wouldn't do for him. I knew if the situation was reversed, Danny would have done the same.

"That had to be hard on you. Having to step up at a young age to take care of a small child. You would have missed out on your own childhood."

I gave a small shrug as I spoke. "I didn't have a typical childhood, but I wouldn't have had one to begin with. My parents were very picky about who we could be friends with and what we could do with our free time. We didn't get to be normal teenagers or kids, really. We didn't get to have sleepovers. We didn't get to go and hangout at a friend's house or have a friend over. There was no trick or treating, no Easter Bunny, not even Santa Claus. We were always told from a young age that they didn't exist.

Christmas was about honoring Jesus and it wasn't designed to receive gifts, but to give back. Birthdays were not celebrated. I used to sneak Danny in a cupcake and a present on his. I knew it wasn't normal, so I tried my best to give Danny the most normal life I could."

Growing up with my parents messed me up and I didn't want that to happen to Danny, it's why I protected him as best as I could. I didn't want him to be a nineteen year old virgin scared to have his first kiss and having no idea if he was attracted to women or men. Yes, now I knew, and I had gotten my first kiss, but it wasn't a life I wanted him to have.

"You said *punished* if something was right. Could you talk a bit about that?" he asked, gently.

"They never hit us, they could never risk someone seeing a mark on us. But they would hurt us in other ways. Sometimes, it would be locking us in our room for twenty some odd hours if we didn't look proper enough, or if we said something they considered embarrassing. They used to keep Danny up in his room when they had dinner parties because he never liked the food and to them that was shameful on them. If we got the floor dirty or accidentally broke a dish, we were to scrub the floor with a toothbrush all over the house until they were satisfied. If we got a bad grade, we would be forced to stand with our back against the wall in a squat position and have to hold our arms out straight with ten pounds in our hand. We were told not to move until they said we had learned our lesson. Sometimes, it was only an hour, but one time Danny got an eighty on a test and not a hundred and he had to stand there for six hours. I tried to cover up for him as best as I could. Whenever he made a mess or broke something, I would say I did it to protect him from their volatile words and punishments."

I was sure to some people the punishments weren't that extreme. They never hit us. They never raised their hand to us, or threw anything at us. They didn't have to in order to control or abuse us. Their words and actions did that all on their own. It's why I worked my ass off to get out of that house on my eighteenth birthday and, thankfully, Danny was here with me now, and hopefully, he would never have to go back to them.

"I'm sorry that happened to you, to the both of you. Growing up, it's not supposed to be that hard. I can put you in touch with a great therapist should you or Danny ever want to talk about it," Travis offered.

"I appreciate that. I'm good, but I'll mention it to him and see."

I didn't need to talk to a shrink about my childhood, but maybe Danny wanted to. I would never want to make him feel like he couldn't reach out and speak to a professional. Just because I didn't believe in it or feel like I needed to, I didn't want Danny to feel like he had to have the same belief.

"Danny has been here for almost nine months, now. How did that transpire?"

"One night Danny decided to come

out to our parents. I wasn't aware of it, and had I known he was planning on telling them, I would have made sure to be there for it. He told them over dinner and our father got very upset with him and threw him out. Danny always knew he could come live here with me. It's why I made sure to have a two bedroom apartment. They haven't tried to contact him since that night. Whenever they have gotten a hold of me, they don't ask about him. Up until recently, Danny was dead to them."

"But recently they have changed their mind and are looking to send him away, you said in your court complaint."

"Yes, they want to send him to a conversion therapy camp for homosexual males. I can't let that happen to him."

"No one wants that to happen to any

child. Those camps are illegal and need to be shut down. You did the right thing by filing within the courts. I am going to speak with both of your parents within the next couple of days and see what they say transpired growing up and with their allegations. I will be doing a thorough investigation and I will only make my recommendation once I am confident in who would be best to care for Danny."

"But he can stay here, though, right until you do?"

I didn't even think about what would happen while the court case was going on. I had assumed he would be with me, but I had no idea social services would be involved, either.

"Yes, he will remain here with you until a ruling has been made. I don't see the need to remove him from the home that you have provided for him. You're doing a good job, Thad," he said warmly.

"Thank you," I said back with my own small smile.

"It was nice to meet you, Thad. I am sorry that it had to be under this type of circumstances," he said as he held his hand out for me.

I easily took it, but I noticed that he had some bruising all along his wrist as his dress shirt moved up just slightly.

"You as well. Are you okay?" I asked, referring to the bruising.

"Oh yeah, I was not born with grace. My parents used to joke about having to put a helmet on me," he said, flashing me a grin as he stood.

"Social suicide," I commented as I stood as well.

He chuckled at that. "Thankfully, my parents never held up their end of the threat. I just avoid doing anything that requires a good deal of coordination."

"That's probably for the best."

"Okay, I will get in contact with your parents and speak with them. I will be back to speak with you and Danny in two weeks. By then, Danny will have a rough idea of what he is feeling from everything going on with the court case. I am assuming you have told him about it."

"I did, yes. I am keeping the bulk of the details away from him, but he does know why I filed."

"And that is fine. He doesn't need to know all of the nitty gritty stuff, just the important aspects of the case. If something comes up, don't hesitate to call me," he said as he handed me his business card, which I took and flashed a small smile back.

"Thank you."

It wasn't until Travis was gone before I could finally take a deep breath and breathe once again. The meeting hadn't gone as badly as I thought it would. He seemed like a nice guy and he seemed very understanding of our situation. He wasn't taking Danny out of the house or talking as if I was a terrible brother and guardian.

I had no idea what my parents were going to say. I knew it wasn't going to be easy and all of this would not be over and done with at the next court hearing. But I was hoping that maybe Travis would side with me and Danny and my parents could finally leave us the hell alone. With this meeting out of the way, I could head into work and get some things done there. I was also going to be meeting up with Jay tonight, something I was both nervous and excited for. I still wasn't sure it was a good idea to be messing around with him, but my body wanted him and, for once in my life, I was going to be selfish and do something that made me feel good. I just hoped it wouldn't all blow up in my face.

***

Jay opened the door and let me in. I was nervous, but I also knew I didn't have to be. He made the kiss feel good and I knew he would be able to make anything else feel good. Still, it was nerve wracking not really knowing what was going to happen.

RESCUE

When I texted him this morning asking for another lesson, I wasn't really sure he would even say yes. I was also horny and had woken up after the most amazing erotic dream. I was in a different mindset than I currently was. Texting was easy because you didn't have to see the person while you said all of those things.

He let out a warm chuckle as he closed the door. "Relax, I don't bite."

He was teasing, but I wasn't entirely certain he didn't bite. I had asked for this, so I shouldn't be nervous, but my mind wasn't getting the message that my body was screaming at it.

I wanted him.

Even standing here and seeing him, I wanted his body. My body was already tingling with the need to feel his lips against my own. With the need to feel his skin against my own. My mind just needed to get on board and stop trying to ruin the very little fun I'd had in my life.

"Sorry," I said as I tried to shake off the nerves.

He spoke as he guided me into his living room and over to his couch. "It's natural to be feeling anxious and nervous. Everyone is the first time they move things along. Remember, we don't have to do anything that you aren't ready for. We'll go as slow as you need."

The sincerity in his voice helped to ease some of my nerves. He was a truly sweet guy and he made sure I was in control of the pace we set.

"I appreciate that."

"How was the meeting today?" he

asked, changing the subject for me, and I was grateful for it.

"It was better than I was expecting. Travis Manning is my social worker and he seemed like a very nice man. He's a not much older than me, so I guess he's pretty new. He is going to let Danny live with me while the court case is going on. He was going to interview my parents and then come back in two weeks to talk with Danny."

"Good. That's good. I've never heard of Travis Manning, but I don't know every social worker in the city. The two weeks is good. It will force the court to wait until Travis has finished going through his investigation. It buys us more time."

I just gave a nod. It was good to hear, but it also was hard to sit here with him on the couch and not do anything. A fire was building up inside of me and I thought I might explode. I couldn't help but look at his lips. I swear, I could already feel them against my own. I was already half-hard and all we had done was sit here on his couch.

This was insane.

Absolutely insane.

Jay leaned in and started to close the gap between our bodies.

"You keep looking at my mouth. See something you want?"

"I don't know what is happening with me," I softly admitted.

"Your body has been starved of pleasure and now it's starting to unlock. Your body is craving pleasure. It's building up, like a volcano, and it's just waiting to erupt." He closed the gap between us, our lips just a hair away from touching. "Let it erupt."

And with that, his lips were pressing against mine and I was instantly responding. The fire that was tickling my skin grew and I knew what he had said was true, my body was craving the pleasure that another man could give me and it wanted it desperately.

I kissed him back hungrily and slipped my tongue into his mouth the first second that I could. He easily allowed me to have a bit more control this time, and I was taking full advantage of it. The passion between us was hotter than the last time we kissed, on both of our parts. I could feel Jay's need for more as desperately as my own.

He moved first, placing his hands on the hem of my shirt and pulling it up.

We broke apart just long enough for us to rid the other of their shirt, before Jay's lips were back on mine.

He pushed his weight toward me and guided me down onto the couch so I was lying down. He placed himself between my legs, which I easily opened for him. I had no idea what was taking over me, but the need to feel him against me was greater than anything I had ever felt before.

The second our dicks touched, I let out a deep moan as pleasure shot right through me. Jay broke the kiss and started to kiss his way down my neck as he ground his hardness against me. I couldn't help but moan as he rubbed against me. I moved my hands along his bare back and down to his ass.

"Jay," I moaned as he started to suck

on my neck.

"That's it, just feel, Baby," he said as he moved his hand to my belt.

The pleasure was all consuming and I never wanted it to end. Jay got my belt open and started to work on my pants. The need to feel his dick in my hand was too powerful to ignore. I moved my hands and started to get his pants open and once we both had the other free of their pesky pants, his hand was sneaking into my boxers and pulling my dick out.

The second his hand made contact with my dick, the pleasure skyrocketed and I cried out.

It felt amazing.

He felt amazing.

I wrapped my hand around his hard cock as he started to kiss me once again.

He began to move his hand up and down my shaft and I mimicked his movements. I was rewarded by a moan from him and it was the sweetest sound I had ever heard.

I had no idea how long we spent touching each other and making out, but when a deep heat in the pit of my stomach started to build, I knew I was close. I could feel his dick getting harder in my hand and I knew he was right with me. We both picked up our pace and had to stop kissing from the moans and panting we were both doing.

"You're close. Come for me, Baby," he said as he brushed his lips over my neck and started to suck on it once again.

The added sensation of his mouth on my neck was enough to push me over the edge.

"Jay," I cried out, followed by a long, low groan as the heat from my stomach erupted and I was swimming in a hot wave of pleasure as I came hard and long. The pleasure was so strong, that I couldn't even keep my hand going to bring Jay over the edge. All I could feel was rope after rope of my own scorching cum hitting my stomach. I didn't think it would ever end. My mind was just able to register that Jay was pumping his hips into my hand so he could finish himself. I tightened my hand slightly and the deep groan of appreciation that bubbled from his lips told me that he loved it. He was shooting his load a moment later and his cum joined mine on my stomach.

The only sound in the house was that of our panting. If I thought my body had been tingling from his kisses, it was nothing compared to what I felt right now. I felt like I had been denied oxygen for hours. My whole body was floating and my head felt all funny. I guess it had been from all of the panting and moaning. Jay placed one last kiss to my neck before he pulled up a bit as he spoke.

"You okay?"

"That was amazing."

I can't believe I had denied myself this type of pleasure for so long. That I had allowed my parents to dictate who I was supposed to be. If I'd had the chance growing up to explore who I was, I would have discovered that I was gay and I could have experienced this level of pleasure instead of being denied it.

"And it only gets better," he said,

flashing me a cocky grin as he started to stroke me again. "I'm not about to let you go anytime soon, Baby."

His lips claimed mine once again and I submitted to him. I had no idea we would be doing this more than once, but I was not about to stop him. Tonight was all about pleasure and I was all too happy to keep playing with him.

CHAPTER EIGHT

Jay

IT'D BEEN ONE month since the first
court hearing and today we were back in
court. I was supposed to have something
that would show proof that Mr. Smythe
was trying to get Danny within a
conversion camp. So far, I had nothing.

I knew Damien and Sebastian
were working hard on trying to get any

type of evidence that they could, but I also knew it wasn't instant. If Craig and Mr. Smythe were covering their asses, it would take time to find something actionable.

Damien and Sebastian were good, they were one of the best firms I had worked with and I believed they would find me something. It just wasn't going to be in time for this court hearing, which meant I needed to try to postpone it once again before we moved further. My main concern was Ken. He was not going to tolerate this being postponed for much longer. He had a lot of money on the line to get this wrapped up within the next thirty days.

"What happens today?" Thad asked me as we stood outside the courtroom waiting to be called in.

"Judge Wilson will ask about any evidence that we have to show that your parents are looking to send Danny away."

"And you found some?" he asked, hopeful.

I hated this part, having to tell my client that I didn't have what the judge wanted or needed. It wasn't a good feeling and, thankfully, it didn't happen very often. Normally, it might not be that big of a deal. The judge would postpone it another thirty days to give me the chance to gather the proper evidence. However, with Ken being Thad's parents' lawyer, it wasn't going to go over well. He wasn't going to leave this to be dragged out. He was going to push for a ruling and I wasn't confident that Judge Wilson wouldn't agree.

"Not yet. We will, but as of this moment we don't have any proof."

"So what do we do?" he asked, now clearly very worried.

"I'm going to try and postpone it again another thirty days. I am also going to use the constant phone calls to try and get a no contact order. I need to put up roadblocks that forces their lawyer to have to deal with those things first."

"Will that work?"

"I don't know. Look, worse case scenario and the final court hearing is scheduled for next week, Danny is still sixteen. He gets to say who he wants to live with. Plus, social services is still involved and they haven't made a ruling yet, either, on who would be better for him. That has to be figured out first before a final hearing, so we still have a bit of time."

That was our only saving grace. Travis had to look into his parents and see how they were living and how they felt toward Danny being gay. He had to do his own investigation and he couldn't make an official stance until it was completed.

Judge Wilson needed that before he could make a ruling. It could delay things by a couple of weeks, but I wanted longer. I wanted the time to investigate the camp and make sure that Danny would never have to go into it.

Looking over at Thad, I could see the worry all over his face. He didn't like having things so much up in the air, not that I could blame him. This wasn't a position that I wanted to be in, either. I hated that I couldn't have better news for him right now. I wished I could have told him that we had everything we needed and that things could be over and done with today.

Unfortunately, that wasn't the case and it wouldn't be even if we did have the evidence. The court system didn't work that way. It was frustrating for me, so I could only imagine how frustrating it was for him.

Our names were called, so we made our way into the courtroom. We took our seats and, like last time, Ken made his way in after us. What was different, though, was Thad's parents were with him.

Thad hadn't seen or spoken with his parents since the night they shared a meal together and he discovered what their plan was. They had called him over two hundred times within the past thirty days and I knew they wanted to try and convince him that Danny going to conversion therapy was best for him. I had told Thad to ignore the calls and save all of the voicemails so we could use them in court, should we need to. That day might come today, depending on how this hearing went.

I could see Thad tensing up at the sight of his parents and I hated that I couldn't comfort him like how I wanted to. I would have loved to take him in my arms and tell him it all would be okay, but I couldn't.

Not just professionally, but on a personal level, too. I had no idea if it all would be okay. I had no idea how this case was going to turn out. I knew what

I wanted to happen and we did have a backup plan should this one fail, but that was also not a guarantee. We were playing against time and, unfortunately, that didn't always work.

Judge Wilson walked in and once again we all stood. Once he was seated, I had Thad sit as I stood, knowing that me and Ken would be going back and forth on this.

"Good morning, today we are to hear evidence of the allegations behind the conversion camp. Mr. Dawson, what do you have?" Judge Wilson started.

"Good morning, your Honor. I have been working on collecting evidence for you on this matter. I have found the leader of the conversion camp and I did sit down with him, but as you can imagine, he is being extremely cautious with releasing any information. We are still gathering intel."

"They have nothing, your Honor. And my clients shouldn't be punished because Mr. Dawson is incapable of securing the information that he claims to be out there. My clients are respectable members of society and they are very active in church. They do not deserve to have their name dragged through the mud. We are pushing to have this issue resolved today and to have Danny back home where he belongs."

"Your Honor, as you know, Child Protective Services is still in the middle of their active investigation. A ruling can't be made until they have completed their investigation and can confidently rule on where the better placement would be for Danny. Danny is also sixteen and not six. He has every right to speak up for himself and make an informed decision on where he would like to live as well. It's unrealistic for Mr. Arnold to demand for this case to be ruled on today."

That was beyond true and I knew Judge Wilson would agree. He wouldn't rule on this today, but I was hoping to get enough time to be able to gather more information on the camp and their connection to the Smythe's.

"Enough, counselors. Mr. Arnold, I appreciate your interest in wrapping things up quickly, but Mr. Dawson is correct. Until social services have submitted their recommendation on where Danny should live, this case cannot be ruled. I also would like to sit down with Danny and speak with him myself and see how he is feeling. He is sixteen and his feelings on who he wants to live with hold a good deal of weight within the court. The next court date will be two weeks from now. That should give social services enough time to complete their investigation and for me to speak with Danny in this matter," Judge Wilson stated.

"Your Honor, I would like to submit a claim for a no contact order between the Smythe's and both of their children. The Smythe's have called my client within the past month over two hundred times and have left just as many voicemails. Some of which have been threatening. I have the phone records of those calls as well as voicemail saved onto a flashdrive for the court."

"My clients are rightfully concerned for the welfare of their youngest son," Ken interrupted.

"They didn't hold any concern for the welfare of the child when they kicked him out at fifteen for being gay. They also have not reached out to Danny over the first eight months he lived with my client. It's only been since this court case was filed have they now decided to call, endlessly. And they are not calls made during the day, but after midnight when they know both my client and his brother would be sleeping. Not to mention, not once in any of the voicemails they have left have they even asked about Danny and how he was doing. They are all threatening in nature and abusive toward my client. I don't think a no contact order is an unreasonable request, your Honor."

"All right, gentlemen, that is enough," Judge Wilson started as he held his hand up to silence whatever Ken was about to counter. "Mr. Dawson, submit the phone logs and the flashdrive to the court. We will make a copy of it so Mr. Arnold will have it for his clients. I am going to agree to a no contact order. Even you, Mr. Arnold, would have to agree that even a hundred phone calls within thirty days would be excessive, let alone two hundred."

"Your Honor, we would like to petition to have the child in question removed from the current home and placed within a foster home until social services have completed their investigation," Ken started.

"What?" Thad shouted out as he

stood up.

I placed my hand on his shoulder and pushed him back down as I spoke. "On what grounds?"

"Your client works over a hundred hours a week and when he is not working he is sleeping. Leaving the child in question unsupervised all day and night long. It has been on the child to cook meals for himself. The child in question has been more of a parent than Mr. Dawson's client."

"The child in question is sixteen and not three. Legally, he is allowed to be alone at home during the day. The child in question, also volunteers eight hours a day outside of the home where he is supervised and getting proper social interaction. My client works so many hours to provide a suitable home for his younger brother, plus have money saved up to help pay for post secondary education. He's not out doing drugs and drinking his money away." It pissed me off that Ken wanted to play that card. Like a foster home would be better for a sixteen year old gay kid. I knew what the foster system was like and I was not about to let that happen to him.

"Calm down, Mr. Dawson. The child in question will remain in the care of his brother. He has been there for nine months now, eight of which your clients, Mr. Arnold, allowed him to stay there. They knew the hours their older son worked and I know that for a fact. Young Mr. Smythe has been working at that mechanic shop since he was fifteen. His parents are well aware of the hours he puts in."

The door to the courtroom opened and we all turned to see who it was. This was a closed courtroom with it being in regard to a minor, so no one was supposed to come in.

I saw Damien walking in with a folder in his hand. He was also not wearing a suit, but just black jeans, a black t-shirt, and his leather jacket. I always suspected he had a motorcycle as well, but he never let it slip that he did or that he knew how to ride one.

"This is a closed courtroom," Judge Wilson started, and I could hear that he was annoyed.

"My apologies, your Honor, but this is something you need to see. It's in regard to this case," Damien said as he walked forward and handed me the file.

I opened it and saw some intel on the

camp. A quick flip through told me what I needed to know. I turned back to the judge, who did not look happy, and spoke.

"Your Honor, this is Damien Anderson, a private detective that I hired to look into the conversion camp owner, Craig Brooks. I will submit this to the court, but there are photos of Brooks and Mr. Smythe meeting together. There are also emails between the two speaking about when he can go and view the camp and how it all works. Brooks explains the process of conversion therapy and some of their therapeutic treatments."

"All of which would have been obtained illegally. I have not been given a warrant for any of those records," Ken started.

"Did you obtain a warrant, Mr. Dawson?" Judge Wilson asked.

"There was no need for a warrant, your Honor. I did surveillance to obtain the photos, all of which are taken in a public place and date and time stamped. The emails were done through a local business' wifi. They keep a record of everything that transpires on their wifi, and when I asked if I could view it the owner granted me permission. There was no warrant needed," Damien answered.

That is why Damien was the best. He knew exactly how to skate around the law without touching the illegal side of it. He was also one hell of a talker and I knew that owner would have given Damien anything he wanted. All he would have had to do was ask for it.

"He's right, Mr. Arnold, everything he

collected is admissible in court. Given the new found evidence, I am going to postpone the next hearing until thirty days from now. I need time to review and so will social services," Judge Wilson easily said.

"Your Honor, this is ridiculous. There's no reason why this can't be resolved within a week. These allegations are false and their so called evidence doesn't even point to a conversion camp or that my client wanted to send his son there." Ken was not happy about the delay for thirty days, putting him right in the category of *goodbye bonus*.

"Well, Mr. Arnold, if my ruling is unfair and ridiculous as you have stated, I apologize. I was not aware of how valuable your time was. Allow me to correct that by having the new court hearing forty-five days from now. Would you care to keep talking and make it sixty?"

I had to fight to keep the smirk off from my face. Judge Wilson was not in the mood for the big city slicker to come in and try and control his courtroom. What Ken said in a big city might not have been that big of a deal, but down here, the judges really didn't like it when you gave them lip of any kind.

Ken just simply shook his head and I could no longer contain the smirk. Once the judge hit his gavel, we were cleared to leave. I once again waited until Ken and his clients left before I nodded to Damien and Thad to follow me out. We walked out and once again got into my car to ensure no one would over hear us.

"You're a detective?" Thad asked

Damien.

"Private detective, it's like a private investigator, but I can do a bit more within the court," he explained.

"Where do we go from here?" I asked Damien, referring to the camp.

"Sebastian is tailing him. He's bound to go to the camp at some point. He's keeping a log of every building he goes into and photographing every person he meets with and their cars. I am going to get a warrant with the intel that I gathered, to dig into his financials and we can see what he's paying where. A camp has to generate bills. That money is coming from somewhere."

"Follow the money," I said with complete understanding.

"It always takes you to where you want to go. Once we find the location of the camp, I'll reach out to a friend of mine who is a Fed. He'll be able to send a team down to shut the camp down for good and arrest everyone there. We'll need a social worker that we can trust."

"I don't know of one off by hand. I've dealt with some pretty questionable ones. Try Travis Manning, he's the social worker for Danny, dig into him and let's make sure he's on the right side of things. If he is, reach out and let him know what you found and what we'll need when we get the camp shut down."

"I'll dig him out. I'll let you know when we have something," Damien said, before he went and climbed out of my car.

"You didn't tell me you were going to hire a private detective. Don't I have to sign off on it?" Thad asked, once we were alone.

"Normally, but Damien isn't charging me for this so there's no charge to you. He does crimes against children for free. He'll get us what we need to keep Danny with you, and he will make sure we have the evidence to shut the camp down. I know today didn't go exactly smoothly, but we do have forty-five days, now, to keep building a case against them. That's a guaranteed forty-five days of Danny being with you. It's a win."

I didn't want him to feel discouraged by how today went. It was a win. A small win, but a win, nonetheless. He needed to celebrate the wins and to look at things on the bright side by having Danny still with him.

"Yeah, okay. I gotta get to work. I'll message you later maybe?"

"Anytime."

I gave him a warm smile before he, too, climbed out of my car. The other night was fun and I was looking forward to the next time he wanted another lesson. He was good and I knew he would only get better with practice. For now, though, I had to head back to the office and go through everything that Damien had found so far. If we wanted this camp shut down, we were going to have to be the ones to do it.

CHAPTER NINE

Thad

"THANKS," I SAID as I took the offered beer.

I was back over at Jay's house for some fun time together. We had both been working hard, me at work and him on his cases, so we hadn't been able to get together for the past two weeks. Not being able to see him for the past two weeks had been harder than I was expecting. It wasn't even the sexual experiences between us that had me missing him, it was the conversations that we shared. I was enjoying getting to know him on a personal level.

"You know about what my childhood was like, what about you?" I asked, looking to see if I could get more information out of him.

He had been pretty open about past cases, the ones that he could talk about, and anything that he had done in law school and after he graduated. The thing he didn't seem to talk about was his childhood and I couldn't help, but be curious about it. He knew all about mine with him being my lawyer, not that it bothered me. I wasn't traumatized by my childhood and I wasn't trying to hide anything. It wasn't the most loving and caring environment, but others had it a lot worse than we did. Apparently, Jay fit in that category if the pain that flashed across his eyes was any indication.

"I'm sorry, I didn't mean to ask you something that would be upsetting. It's okay," I instantly said, hating that I had put that pain inside of him.

"No, it's okay. I don't really talk about it. It wasn't a happy childhood, but it made me the man that I am today. I grew up in the foster system and went through some horrible homes. When I was twelve, I actually met an eight year old boy named Chris. He was really shy, didn't even talk. He had been in the system his whole life and had been horribly abused in previous homes. I took to him and he became my kid brother. We were so close that the social workers knew we had to be placed together in every home. When I was sixteen, we were placed in a foster home with very strict and religious parents. I knew I was gay and Chris had discovered he was gay as well. We had kept it hidden as best as we could in the homes. Some of the older guys in the homes, they didn't have a problem with getting head or having sex with a guy. To them, it was a hole they could put their dick in. Whenever someone suspected Chris of being gay, I would cover for him. Our foster father suspected we were gay and he sent us both to a conversion camp."

"You've been in a camp?"

The wave of pain that crashed into my chest was staggering. I had no idea he had any personal experience with being in a place like that. I had been so worried about Danny and what he could go through if he was trapped there, I never even thought to ask how Jay felt about working this case. I didn't think he would have any personal experiences that could cause him harm working my case.

"Yeah, for six months we were in it together. It was really bad and I tried to shield Chris from it, but they kept us separated as often as they could. One night, Chris couldn't take it anymore and he hung himself. His body was found the next morning and the camp leader decided to use it as a way to teach me a lesson. He made me bury him. That night, I escaped and told the police where the camp was and it was shut down."

"Oh my god. I'm so sorry."

I couldn't even imagine what he had felt at the time. To go through something so horrific, I couldn't imagine. Somehow, after everything he went through, he still became a lawyer and has been dedicated to helping children be in a safe place. It was inspiring, but it would also trigger memories for him, memories that he would have to continuously work through.

"It's okay. It's hard to talk about, but I've worked through it."

"Where did you go once you got out?" He would only have been sixteen. He would have had two more years before he would be allowed to be on his own.

"I actually had received an early acceptance into law school. I had been working hard in high school to graduate early and get away. I was taking courses during the summer and extra courses throughout the year to graduate in two instead of four. It was a lot of work, but it also got me out of the house for the majority of the time. When I got there, I was sixteen and the youngest in the school. I had gotten into the wrong crowd pretty quickly and, by the end of the first month, I was using drugs and partying every Friday and Saturday night. I was still getting good grades and doing my assignments, but I was more interested in getting high whenever I could. I had a professor who took an interest in me, and not in a good way, but I was so messed up from what happened and the drugs I didn't see it right away. We became fuck buddies and he encouraged me to use, even held my arm and shot me up with heroin. I was with him and used until I was twenty."

Wow, just wow. That was not what I was expecting at all. I don't know what I was expecting, but him to be an intravenous drug user was not it. It was unreal. Sitting here looking at him now, you would have no idea. He clearly had been through some traumatic experiences and it all exploded on him once he was away from the abuse. His professor was clearly a piece of work, for him to manipulate and abuse him like that. And to think he was a professor, someone that was supposed to be a lawyer and there to help people. He was disgusting and he deserved a special place in hell for what he had done. There was no doubt he had done this to other students before and after Jay.

"How did you get clean?" I asked.

"In my last year of law school, there was a professor that took notice of me. He could see the signs as he himself had been a drug addict. He grew up in the system, as well, and we really clicked. He helped me to get sober without me having to lose the school year. It was hard, but I got through it. I lived with him and for the next year he helped me to start to heal from everything that happened to me. He became my mentor and, once I graduated, he helped me to decide what I wanted to do with my new life. I decided to face all of my fears and trauma head on by helping children in the foster system and in bad homes to be safe. He loaned me money to get the firm up and running."

"He sounds like a great man. I'm sorry you went through all of that. I couldn't imagine going through any of it, let alone all of it. You're incredibly strong and brave. He must be really proud of you."

The fact that he could go through so much trauma and still come out stronger on the other side. It was remarkable and truly spoke to the level of strength that he had inside of him. I knew some people would be worried about his past, about the drug use, but I knew people could change and I was not about to judge him based on his past. That wasn't fair and I wouldn't want anyone to judge me based on my past. Sure, there wasn't much you could judge me on, but it wouldn't be fair, either way. The man that was sitting here in front of me was a good man, well on his way to being a great man. That was all that mattered.

I could tell he needed the break from conversation, from the emotional pain that it brought up. I hated that the conversation had turned this way. I wasn't looking to cause him any harm, I was just curious about him, and wanted to get to know him a bit more.

I knew this was only for fun, that when we'd started this we both weren't looking for anything serious. We were only having fun with each other, no strings attached, and I knew that was what he wanted. I was confident that it had been what I wanted as well, but the more time I spent with him, the more I wanted to get to know him. I was starting to develop deep feelings for him and I wasn't certain that was the smartest thing to do in the world.

I had never been in a true relationship before and I had no idea how to even have one. He probably wasn't interested in anything outside of the fun we had been having, but with the lack of social interactions growing up, I didn't know how to read any tells that he would want more. I was putting myself in a position to be hurt down the road when Jay decided it was time to move on.

Pushing those thoughts out of my head, I forced myself to focus on this moment. The time that I was getting to share with him and not what the future could hold. I had to learn how to live in the moment and that is exactly what I was going to do.

Moving confidently, I straddled his lap and pressed my lips against his. Instantly, he responded to me and placed one hand on the side of my face and his other on my ass, pulling me closer to him. I could feel his need for a distraction, for a release of the emotional pain he was in. I couldn't blame him and I was more than willing to be that distraction.

Our hands quickly worked at the other's shirt, getting them off and leaving me the freedom to run my hands along his toned chest. He placed both of his hands on my ass and we started to grind against each other. The need for the other was too strong and we both needed more than just the small contact we were getting.

In one swift movement, Jay picked

me up from the bottom of my ass and I wrapped my legs around his waist. We continued to kiss as he guided us up the stairs and into his bedroom. I had never been in his room before, but I was far too distracted to be looking around it, now.

Jay laid me down on his bed and my hands went straight for his pants. We worked quickly to strip the other naked and I easily opened my legs as he settled between them. The second our hard dicks touched we both let out a deep moan.

After a few more minutes of making out and dry humping, Jay broke the kiss and spoke in that husky voice that he always got after an intense make out session.

"You want another lesson?"

I knew what the next lesson would be. It would be oral sex and, originally, I was a bit freaked out by it, but right now in this moment, I wanted nothing more than to feel his mouth on me.

To feel him in mine.

"Fuck yes," I answered.

I had no idea what to do, but it couldn't be all that hard right?

Like eating a popsicle, but without the teeth portion.

My agreement was all Jay needed to hear before he was moving. He lay down on his side, but he did so in the opposite direction as me so we were more head to toe than face to face.

"Turn and face me," he instructed.

I easily did as he said and our new positions put us both at the right height for the other's dick.

"Just do what I do," Jay said, before he gave my shaft a long lick, causing me to moan.

If I hadn't been hard to begin with, I would have definitely been, now. I forced my mind to focus and to move, giving Jay a long lick up his shaft, just like he did to me.

I was surprised to discover that I didn't get any taste on my tongue. I don't know what I was expecting, I had never done oral with a guy or a girl before, but I guess I always figured there would be a taste of some sort. The taste didn't come until I mimicked him and sucked on his tip, then a sweet taste hit my tongue and, instantly, I wanted more.

I allowed my body and instincts to take over and I stopped waiting for Jay to do something first. The feel of him in my mouth, moving along my tongue, was unlike anything I had ever felt before. This was something I could get addicted to. The second I heard him moan, I wanted more. To know that I could drive him this crazy with just my mouth, it was intoxicating.

The only thing that was making this out of the world, was feeling his mouth on me. I couldn't believe I had denied myself this level of pleasure for so long. It was a true disservice that I had done to myself and I was not about to make that mistake again.

The pleasure quickly grew within the both of us. The need for the other was getting explosive. I could feel him hardening in my mouth and I knew what that meant. I thought I would be bothered by the idea of a guy coming in my mouth, but at this moment, I wanted nothing more than to taste everything that he had for me.

We both picked up our pace, taking the other all of the way down to the base. I was the one to break first and I gave a long, low moan around his dick as I came hard. The vibrations that I sent down his dick was apparently enough to send him over the edge and I was rewarded with his sweet taste flooding my mouth. I did my best to swallow around him in my mouth and I continued to suck and lick his tip until I got every last drop.

We both released the other and turned to lie down on our backs, both of us breathing heavily. My body was tingling and I loved it. Jay was remarkable, absolutely remarkable, and

I was really glad that I had taken the chance to explore with him.

"I liked that lesson," I said, flashing him a big goofy smile.

Jay let out a chuckle at that. "You're a natural."

It made me feel good to hear that he enjoyed what I did with him, to him. I was still uncertain about all of this, with it being new. It helped to hear that I was doing something right.

Jay moved so he was now face to face with me and he pulled me in for a slow and gentle kiss. The taste of myself on his tongue flooded my mouth and I found it didn't bother me. We slowly kissed for a little while, giving our bodies the chance to become less sensitive before we would go again. Tonight, I was going to enjoy every ounce of his body for as long as I could.

CHAPTER TEN

Jay

HEADING INTO ALIAS Investigations the next morning, I couldn't help but think about last night. Spending time with Thad, talking to him about Chris and my own experiences, it was more than I was expecting. I thought we would just be messing around, having fun, but the deep and meaningful conversations were not at all what I was expecting.

I was the poster boy for no strings attached. I didn't want strings. Strings involved feelings and things get messy, people get hurt, and I didn't want any of that. I didn't want to know what it felt like to be in love. I didn't want to experience heartache. I had gone through enough pain growing up and losing Chris, I didn't want anymore to go with it.

Yet, last night I had spoken to Thad about Chris. I had told him about him, told him secrets that I had been planning on taking to my grave. If that wasn't bad enough, he had slept over and we cuddled. I had cuddled with someone. I had a firm no cuddling, no breakfast rule. There were no sleepovers. Once we were both satisfied, the other left. It was just that simple.

So why the hell had I felt the need to have him around me?

I needed to figure out my own thoughts and feelings toward Thad, but for today, I had to put it all on the backburner and focus on the case. I didn't have just Danny's life riding on the outcome of this custody case, but the kids that were trapped in that conversion camp. They were all waiting for someone to come in and rescue them and I was not about to let them down.

I was hoping that Damien and Sebastian had been able to come up with something that we could use. I headed into their office and made my way over to their conference room where I knew they would be set up. I walked in and saw that there were boxes all over the one end of the table and both Damien and Sebastian were in the room.

"I hope this means you have something," I said as I shrugged my jacket off.

"We were able to get a silent warrant for Brooks' financials and to start a wire," Damien answered.

A wire was a type of case that law enforcement would do at times. It was, essentially, twenty-four seven surveillance and monitoring. Everything was recorded in the wire. Every single person Brooks met with would need to be looked up and dug into. Every place he went, every phone call, every email, it all would be logged and tracked to build a solid case. It was the only way for them to be able to gather all of the information that we needed to shut the camp down.

It wasn't just about finding the location, which hopefully the wire would give us, it was about having enough proof to get the kids away from their parents. To get everyone involved in jail, and the wire would give us that. It was a lot of work, though, and the three of us were in for some long ass hours.

"That's good, but it's only the two of you. How are you going to be able to handle the surveillance?"

I could help in the office, but I had my own cases I was working as well. I couldn't follow Brooks around all day.

"We have trusted people that we've pulled in to help keep an eye on him while we are running the intel," Damien answered, before he pointed to the boxes as he continued. "These are all the finances of Brooks. We just started to go through them. He's got a lot of corporations that he is using to bounce money around. It's going to take time to find where it all came from and where the camp is."

"We're hoping one of the locations that Brooks will go to will be the camp," Sebastian added.

"They in a specific order?" I asked, referring to the boxes.

"Nope, paperwork is all over the place. We're in the process of organizing it by date," Damien answered.

I gave a nod and grabbed one of the boxes and got started on it. We had to get the paperwork in order so we could see the timeline. It wouldn't do us any good to focus on old intel. We had to know what was most recent so we could work backward from it.

Most conversion camp owners will change locations after a set amount of years. We needed to know the most recent and then try to find previous locations to search for any evidence or bodies. The extreme conversion camps, like the one I was in, would hide their accidents to ensure they could keep getting funding from local supporters and clients. Whether a child was killed by accident during a therapy session, or they took their own life, neither could come to light and they had to bury the bodies.

We owed it to those children to find them if Brooks was one of those types of camp leaders. Someone could be looking for their child, brother, or friend, and they deserved closure. They deserved to know what the truth was and those children deserved to have a proper burial.

It was a good four hours before Sebastian headed out to help relieve the man that was currently watching Brooks. Once we were alone, I looked over at Damien. I could see that he was in the zone. This was something that he excelled at, building a case.

I had thought he was an outlaw, but seeing him working this case, seeing him knowing the lingo and how to set up a proper wire case, I was starting to question my original thought. Maybe he was a former law enforcement or a federal agent. The man was a giant mystery and if there was one thing I loved, it was a good mystery. The trick would be to get him to open up to me. He was the definition of a closed book and I knew he was living behind a ten inch thick fortified steel wall. I would need a rocket launcher just to make a dent in it. Still, I had to try.

"You and your brother are good at this."

"He's not my brother," Damien instantly said, and the slight edge to his voice told me I was right on track.

"I've known you for a couple of years now, Damien. How long are we really going to keep doing this? I know he's not your best friend, or *just* your best friend, I should say. You two look way too much alike to be anything but brothers. Shit, you could almost be identical twins."

"I don't have a brother," Damien said back. He was not going to give it up, and that was just fine. He knew that I knew, and maybe that would be enough for him to come to me should he ever need to chat.

"You keep going with that. I'm here if you ever need to talk or if you need help. I don't know what your story is, or what you both are hiding from, but I did study more than family law."

I didn't work criminal cases, but that didn't mean I couldn't. I was a lawyer. I could work any type of case that I wanted. I preferred family law because of the children, but I wasn't about to leave a friend twisting in the wind, either. If Damien or Sebastian needed help, I would be there for them.

"Careful, Jay, you almost sound like you care. That would be a string." He said it in a teasing tone, but I could hear the underlying hurt to his voice. He might not be interested in anything serious, but that didn't mean he didn't want a string or two.

Damien was a lot like me, he preferred things to be easy and not get emotionally involved. However, we did differ slightly in the sense that he didn't want just a fuck buddy, he wanted a friend, too. Someone that he could grab a beer with and chat about their problems. I wasn't good with friends, not after growing up.

"I'm not good at that part, you know that," I softly admitted.

"I know, but you can't keep going through life without a friend, without someone in your corner. I know your childhood was shit. I know you lost Chris, someone you considered to be your brother, but he wouldn't want you to be alone forever," Damien said gently.

It was weird hearing the soft tone to his voice. He was a big and rough guy, so hearing him talk gently to anyone just didn't seem to fit him.

"I think I made a mistake."

"You slept with Thad?" he simply asked.

The fact that he knew we were messing around didn't surprise me. The man was too observant for his own good. He picked up every little touch or look. It was as if his mind recorded everything and he never forgot.

"I never sleep with a client, ever. I don't know what it is about him. We haven't even had sex. I didn't know he was gay, but then I saw him at a gay club in the next town over. We started talking and I found out he had never even been kissed. I don't know what came over me, but I couldn't help but kiss him. It was just supposed to be fun, something that would let him explore his sexuality without feeling pressured."

"Makes sense. What changed?" he asked as he leaned against the wall. There was no judgment in his voice and I appreciated it.

"I don't know. Last night, he came over to play and we started talking. I told him about Chris. I don't even know why. I never talk about him. I never tell people about him, about what happened. The only one I've told was you and I was beyond drunk. Afterward, we messed around, and instead of kicking him out afterward, we cuddled and slept. We made breakfast before we both headed out."

I wasn't going to tell him about what

else I talked to Thad about. It was bad enough that I had told Thad, I was not about to let Damien know as well. That was my secret, or it used to be, and I wasn't going to divulge it again.

"Wow, you never do that. Good for you."

"Good? I broke my rule. The one that matters the most. He should never have spent the night," I said as I pushed out of my chair. I had all of this emotion trapped inside of me. I needed to move.

"I know you operate with no strings, but, Jay, you already have strings. You had them when you kissed him because he's your client. There's nothing wrong with wanting to have someone close to you. You've been through a lot, more than I know about. Everyone needs someone in their life that knows them, the good and the bad. It seems like Thad could be that person to you."

But did I want him to be?

Did I want to have someone in my life that I could lose?

I didn't know if I could handle that.

If I could handle it if Thad left me, either by choice, or by death.

I didn't know what was happening to me. I had never had a problem with keeping my rules in place. I never wanted to care for someone, and yet, I could feel it happening with Thad. I could feel myself wanting to spend more time with him. I could feel myself wanting to see him in the mornings and share meals together. I wanted to learn more about him and what he was like. Both growing up, and now, as the man he was growing into being. I wanted to even meet Danny and learn more about him. All of this was new and confusing to me, but it was also terrifying as hell. If I allowed myself to add strings to our relationship, I would be allowing myself to feel for someone for the first time. It was terrifying and I had no idea if I could even do it.

"I don't know if I can," I reluctantly admitted.

"You don't have to propose to him, Jay. Just allow yourself to get to know him, for him to get to know you. You could build something real with him and, based on your actions, it seems like you want that, too. Allow yourself the chance to have something more, and if it doesn't work out, then at least you know you did everything you could to make it work. If it doesn't workout, it'll hurt for a bit, but you will overcome it. Part of life is making connections and allowing yourself to love. That's what makes us human and you should never deny yourself that."

An emotional connection was not something I thought I ever wanted. It wasn't something I thought I could handle, but ever since Thad walked through my office door, I couldn't stop thinking about him.

Maybe Damien was right.

Maybe it was time that I took a chance and allowed myself that human connection.

We could take it slow.

I could take it slow.

See how I felt and build up from there.

We both had a lot we had to learn

about the other and how to handle being in an actual relationship. It was both of our firsts, in that sense, and Thad might not even want to be in one. It was something I could bring up when I was ready.

For now, I needed to focus on what I could solve, this case.

Time would tell what would happen between Thad and me.

CHAPTER ELEVEN

Thad

MY BACK HIT Jay's bedroom door as we stumbled into his room once again. We had long since lost our jackets and our shirts as we made our way up to his bedroom. For the past couple of weeks, we had been enjoying the other's body to its full pleasure.

I was very much enjoying the new

sexual activities we were getting up to. I don't know what it was about tonight, but just oral didn't feel like it would be enough tonight. I had no idea what I wanted, but I was pretty certain I wanted more. What more would be at this point, I didn't know. I figured the next logical step would be sex, but how that was going to happen was still unclear to me. Jay said my body would just know, but right now I had no clue. There were no signals, no feelings, nothing that would indicate I wanted to top or to bottom.

Jay turned us around and the back of his knees hit the bed and we collapsed down onto it. I ended up on top of him for the first time and I had to admit, I liked the position. My hands were instantly going to his pants and Jay followed suit. The second we were skin to skin, we were both moaning at the sensitivity of our bodies. Jay broke the kiss as he spoke in that sexy husky voice of his.

"I need to feel you inside of me."

"You want me to?"

I wasn't sure if that was what he was asking and I had to be sure. I had no idea how to top, but the thought of having sex with Jay made my dick pulse.

"Fuck me, yes. If you want to."

"I don't know how." It seemed like a really stupid thing to say in that moment, but it was the truth.

"I'll show you," he said with a smirk.

And that right there might have been the sexiest thing he had ever said to me. Tonight, I was going to lose my virginity and I couldn't think of a better person to give it to than Jay.

***

I couldn't get this stupid smile off my face. Last night had been amazing, absolutely amazing. I was no longer a virgin and it had actually felt good. I was still worried and unsure if I was a top or a bottom, but last night I knew I was at least a top. I could still be a switch, like Jay, and I might be brave enough to try that with him another day, but for now I was going to enjoy being a top. I was really nervous that Jay wouldn't get pleasure out of it, but he looked very happy during and at the end of it.

Even getting to spend the night with him afterward again felt great. It felt perfect to be in his arms at night. I never thought I would be interested in cuddling, but I had to admit it was almost as good as sex. I was falling for him and I knew that was a dangerous place for me to be, a very dangerous place.

He was the first guy that I had done anything with and I was letting my heart get carried away. I couldn't be one of those people that fell in love with the first person they have sex with. Not to mention Jay and me were still firmly in the friends with benefits category, and he didn't come across as the type of guy that wanted more than that. I needed to enjoy the fun and let it all play out.

I walked up to my front door and instantly I noticed that something was wrong. The door had been kicked in. Fear gripped my throat, making it hard for me to breathe. Someone had broken into my apartment.

Mine and Danny's home.

"Danny," I said on a breath.

I ran into the apartment and noticed that it was trashed, but not in an unorganized way. It looked like someone had gotten into a fight in my living room. The coffee table was crushed, the side table lamp was knocked onto the ground, the pictures on the walls were either knocked down or crooked. It was as if someone had fought with someone throughout the room.

"Danny!" I yelled as I took off down the hallway to his bedroom.

The room didn't look like it had seen violence. His bed wasn't made and I knew he made it every morning, so chances were he was woken up suddenly. His cell phone was beside his bed, plugged in like he always left it when he went to bed. His backpack was in the chair at his desk, his laptop sat closed on his desk. Everything was perfectly in place, like it would be if he was going to bed.

I headed into my room and saw that it was the same as I had left it. I went back into his bedroom and looked at his phone. I quickly pulled up the call log and saw that he never called 9-1-1. The last text was between us when I told him I was going to be out late, that I would see him in the morning. Me telling him I love him and him saying it back.

He never called for help.

He never got the chance.

The bang from the door probably woke him up and he was pulled out of his bed and dragged out into the living room. Danny wasn't much of a fighter, but I had taught him some basic self-defense maneuvers and he must have used them to try to keep from being dragged out of the apartment.

My brother had been kidnapped while I was busy with Jay. I was supposed to be here last night. If I had been here, I would have been able to help protect him, keep him from being taken. It was my fault that he had been kidnapped, probably by someone my parents hired to take him to the conversion camp. I hadn't been here when he needed me the most because I was too busy chasing after my own feelings. Being selfish by sleeping with Jay and spending the night with him. Now, my brother was going through god knows what and I wasn't there to protect him. With a shaky hand I pulled out my phone and called 9-1-1.

"9-1-1, what's your emergency?" The female operator asked.

"I need the police. My brother, he's been kidnapped."

"What's your address, sir?" After I told her she continued. "Okay, the police are on their way. Can you tell me how old your brother is and his name?"

"Danny Smythe. He's sixteen," I said, my whole body was trembling.

"And your name, please?"

"Thad Smythe. I'm nineteen. He's been living with me for almost ten months, now."

"Okay, sir, and why do you suspect he has been kidnapped?"

A sixteen year old kid not being home in the morning wasn't really warranted for a kidnapping complaint, I knew that. But she didn't know the whole story or what this place looked like.

"I was out last night and when I came home the front door was kicked in. The living room, there's evidence of a fight. I went into his bedroom and it's exactly how he leaves it when he goes to bed at night."

"Okay, sir, I'll let the police know. Can I contact your parents for you?"

"No, you can't. We're in a custody battle over Danny. They want to take him to a conversion therapy camp to cure his homosexuality. They probably took him."

There was no official proof that they had anything to do with this, but come on, what more proof do you need besides that?

They wanted him at that camp and I'd been blocking them ever since they'd told me. They could have easily hired someone to grab him and take him. It wouldn't surprise me if they had someone watching me so they would know the best time to grab him.

"All right, sir, I will let the police know. I know it might be hard, but I need you to go and wait in the hallway and not touch anything. If you did touch something, remember it so you can inform the police. They will need to have a crime scene team down there to collect evidence."

"I touched his phone, that was it."

Shit.

I didn't even think about that.

I shouldn't have touched it. The police would have wanted to see everything how it was left.

"That's okay, sir. Let the officers

know when they arrive. I'm going to let you go and if you think of anything, just inform the officers when they arrive. They are already en route to you so they will be there within ten minutes."

"Okay. Thank you."

"You are welcome. I hope you find your brother and I wish you all of the best luck."

I ended the call and moved to stand out in the hallway so I wouldn't disrupt the scene any more than I already had. With a shaky hand I hit Jay's number and put the phone to my ear. The phone kept ringing and for a second I was afraid he wouldn't answer, but he finally did on the fourth ring.

"Miss me already, Baby?"

The sound of his warm voice was enough to bring tears to my eyes that I couldn't contain. I was fighting with the tears to be able to even talk, but every time I tried to say something, all that came out was sobs.

"It's okay, Sweetheart. Take a deep breath for me," Jay said calmly.

I could tell he was worried about why I was calling him crying my eyes out, but I couldn't seem to stop. Everything was hitting me and I couldn't help but feel so guilty over it all. If I had just been here last night, Danny would still be here.

"They took him," I managed to force out.

"Took who, Baby?"

"Danny. They broke in and they took him."

"I'm on my way. You need to call the police," He said and I could hear shuffling of him getting out of bed.

"I did. They're on their way. I'm out in the hallway, the operator said to wait out here."

"Good, that's good, Baby. They need to keep the apartment as clean as possible. The police will want to take some of your DNA and your fingerprints to eliminate you from the apartment. It's completely standard."

"Okay," I said with a shaky voice.

I wasn't worried about them taking my DNA or my fingerprints. It wasn't like I was in the system. Nothing horrible was going to come back on me. Even if there was something, I wouldn't care. Danny was missing and the only thing I cared about was finding him. That was the only thing that mattered. The door to the stairs opened and I saw two police officers walking into the hallway.

"The police are here, I have to go."

"I'm getting in my car now. I'll be there in ten. Just explain to them what you found and answer any questions they have. Try and stay calm and don't get annoyed if they ask you the same thing multiple times," Jay advised.

"Okay, okay. I have to go."

"You got this."

I ended the call and quickly wiped at my cheeks to try and get the tears to stop. It was pointless, but I hoped it would make me appear less crazy. I tucked my phone back into my pocket and turned my attention to the officers. I needed to keep my shit together, Danny was counting on me and every second mattered. I had already failed him last night. I was not about to fail him again.

CHAPTER TWELVE

Jay

THE SECOND I pulled up out front of Thad's apartment, I climbed from my car and ran inside. I had noticed that there were now three patrol cars, one unmarked indicating a detective. I knew a crime scene team would be here, but the closest one was in another town, two hours away. We didn't have one here with the town lacking a serious number of violent crimes.

I took the stairs two at a time until I reached his floor. I had never been here, but I knew his address from the court forms. It also would have been very hard to miss with two officers standing at the hallway entrance in the stairwell.

"Officers, my name is Jay Dawson. I'm Mr. Smythe's lawyer," I said in the most professional voice I could muster at that moment. I knew they weren't going to let me through if they didn't know I was a lawyer. They needed to keep the scene the least contaminated as possible.

"Mr. Smythe is in the manager's office on the first floor, apartment one," the officer supplied.

I gave a nod of thanks before I turned

and made my way back down the stairs. I didn't even think about them placing him somewhere else. It would make sense for them to have him in a quiet place.

The second my feet hit the first floor landing, I pulled open the stairwell door and jogged down the hallway. The manager's office was easy to spot with the hoard of officials in front of the door. I told them who I was before I was allowed to go into the apartment. In the small room was a detective and Thad. Thad was sitting down in a chair with his leg bouncing from anxiety. He looked so small sitting there, defeated, and I hated it. I hated that I couldn't take him in my arms and make this all better.

To take all of it away.

I would be taking him in my arms, of

that there was no doubt, but not until the detective was finished. I knew better than to be unprofessional around law enforcement. I squared my shoulders and walked over to Thad, standing next to him and placing my hand on his shoulder as I spoke.

"Jay Dawson. I am Mr. Smythe's lawyer."

"Detective Hollingsworth. Your client was just informing me of the custody case he is in the middle of."

"Have you sent a patrol over to his parents' house?" I asked.

"I have. No one is home. The patrol unit is going to sit on the house. Your client has provided me with a list of friends that Danny is close with to see if they have heard anything from him or seen anyone lurking around."

"He didn't run away," I instantly said.

There was no way I was going to let anyone assume that Danny staged what happened just so he could run away. He wasn't that type of kid.

"I know, but we do have to look into every possible scenario. I've seen the apartment. I know he didn't run away. Most likely his parents or someone that his parents hired to bring him to the conversion camp grabbed him. Mr. Smythe said you have a private investigator looking into Craig Brooks, the suspected leader of the conversion camp. Do you have anything that I can use?"

The fact that he was willing to work with us, work with a private detective, told me that he was different. I'd had a few run-ins with the local law enforcement, between being in the foster system and running my own firm, and most of them were all the same. They didn't care about the forgotten or troubled children in town. If I had told them that I had a private detective investigating something, they would snub their nose at me and act like Damien was senile. Detective Hollingsworth was apparently more open minded, indicating he was either new and still hopeful in life, or he was from another town.

"I've been working with Damien Anderson and Sebastian Roth. They have a few guys they are working with to keep eyes on Brooks. They were able to secure a warrant to run a wire investigation. They should have possibles for you."

"Perfect. If you can take me there and make the introductions, that would be appreciated."

"Of course," I easily agreed.

"I have to check in with my partner upstairs and then we can head out. Mr. Smythe, I know this is hard for you, but try to not worry. We'll find your brother and make sure whoever is responsible is brought to justice."

"Thank you," Thad said, his voice empty.

I could tell that he was overwhelmed and just done with all of this. Not that I could blame him, it was a lot to come home to.

Detective Hollingsworth headed out, leaving us alone. The second the door closed behind him, I instantly pulled Thad in for a hug. I could feel his body trembling slightly and I knew he was still in a state of shock.

"I'm so sorry," I said, rubbing his back as I held him.

"I should have been here. It never would have happened if I had just been here."

The guilt in his voice was thick and I hated that he was blaming himself for this. Practically his whole life he had been taking care of Danny. He had been denying himself a normal life, working endless hours, just so Danny would have the chance to be a normal teenager. I hated that he was taking the blame for this situation. It wasn't his blame to take on. He had every right to be out for the night. It's not like Danny was a small child. He was a responsible sixteen year old. He could be alone for the night.

"It still would have happened, it just wouldn't have been last night, maybe. But, Babe, it would have happened. They could have grabbed him at a friend's place, on his way to volunteer, or just walking down the road. They weren't going to stop until they grabbed him. Even if you were here last night, they could have hurt you and taken him. We have no idea if they came in armed. You could have been shot and Danny still would have been taken. All we can do is put all of our effort into finding him."

Thad pulled back and wiped at his cheeks. I could tell he was trying to get his mind to focus on what he needed to do, but it was hard. He never expected for his parents to do something like this.

To go this far just to get Danny into

one of those camps.

I knew we were assuming a lot, but the odds of this being unrelated were astronomical. I had better odds of being struck by lightning while getting bit by a shark. This pointed to his parents and that camp. There was no doubt in my mind.

I needed to call Damien to give him the heads up so he could start getting the intel we needed. He would probably still have eyes on Brooks and he might have a photo of Danny's kidnapper or kidnappers.

"I just want to find him," Thad said in a shaky voice.

"And we will. Detective Hollingsworth appears to be taking this very seriously. He wants to meet with Damien and Sebastian to see what they have. That's a good sign. We will find him, I promise you," I said with complete strength in my voice.

I knew for a fact that we would find him. We had enough people watching Brooks, so we had enough potential suspects that we could start running. We knew that Thad's parents were behind this and there would be evidence that they didn't think to hide. We would find it and we would get Danny back and get him justice.

Thad just gave a nod and I could tell he needed a minute. I pulled out my phone and hit Damien's name. He answered after three rings.

"It's early, Jay."

I could hear the exhaustion in his voice. He was most likely up late working my case and I hated that I was about to add on to his plate, but there was no way to avoid it now.

"I'm sorry, but something has happened. Danny's been kidnapped."

"When?" Damien asked, instantly sounding awake.

"Sometime last night. Thad was out. When he came home, the front door had been kicked in. There was evidence of a fight in the living room and Danny wasn't there. He checked his phone, but Danny never called for help."

"Police there?"

"They are. Detective Hollingsworth would like me to bring him to you and Sebastian to see what you have. He seemed very interested in any possibles that you have that could have pulled this off. They sent a patrol to Thad's parents, but they weren't home. The patrol is sitting on the house and, hopefully, they come back soon."

"I'll head to the office and let Sebastian know. We'll get in contact with the guys watching Brooks and see if they have anything for us. We'll start narrowing down who could have taken the kid."

"Do we have an idea of where the camp could be?"

There was no doubt in my mind that Thad's parents took Danny to the camp. We needed to find it, now more than ever, if we were going to stand a chance at locating Danny.

"Not yet. We'll work it and find it. I'll see you soon." Damien ended the call and I tucked my phone back into my pocket.

I hated that I had to leave soon, but I

knew Thad would understand why I was leaving. I had to get Detective Hollingsworth connected with Damien so they could both work this case and find Danny. That was the only thing that mattered right now. There would come a time later for me to comfort Thad and help him deal with his guilt.

I crossed the short distance between us and I placed my hand on his hip as he spoke.

"Did he have anything?"

"Not yet, but they have eyes on Brooks and they are going to start seeing who he spoke with and where he went within the past day or two. They'll find him. They'll find the camp, and we will get Danny home with you where he belongs."

"This never should have happened,"

he said and I could tell the guilt was still strong in him.

"I agree, but that's not on you. It's on your parents and their messed up beliefs. I promise you, though, we *will* find him. Do you want to come with me when I go to see Damien?"

I wasn't certain how involved Thad wanted to be. I knew he wanted to find Danny, but being an active member of an investigation to find him were two very different things. I knew from personal experience how frustrating investigations could be, especially for the family members. It wasn't going to be easy on him. Especially, if we didn't find Danny today. I knew it could take a bit of time, but to explain that to a family member worried sick over their missing loved one was impossible. It had to be his choice and whatever he decided I would support him.

"Of course, I want to be there," he said, his tone slightly defensive, as if I doubted his loyalty to Danny.

"I just wanted to make sure, because it's hard to go through an investigation. I didn't want to pressure you or put you in a position that you didn't want to be in. If you want to be there, then you can be there, and I will support you one hundred percent."

This was not going to be an easy process. It was going to be a long and hard couple of days until we were able to find Danny, most likely at the camp. Even once we did find him, the work didn't stop there. We would have an entire camp to shut down, arrests to make, and children to help. It was going to be a huge undertaking, but one I was not about to back down from.

We would find Danny and we were going to finally shut this camp down once and for all. The biggest mistake that son of a bitch made was taking Danny, and that mistake will be all of their undoings.

CHAPTER THIRTEEN

Thad

FOUR DAYS.

Four horrible and long days since Danny had been kidnapped.

The past four days were all a blur, essentially. I had gone with Jay and Detective Hollingsworth to Alias Investigations and from the second we walked through the door, it'd been nonstop.

It was hard for me to keep up. I had tried, but they all seemed to be speaking some type of language that I never learned. They could have been speaking German, for all I knew.

They all seemed to mesh so well together, though. It was fluid between the four of them. They easily passed information on to one another and they seemed to know exactly what the puzzle was supposed to look like.

It didn't matter to me if I understood everything they were saying or doing, all that I cared about was finding Danny. It didn't take me too long to discover that Danny's best chances were the four men in that conference room.

My parents had surfaced the evening of the first day. They were immediately taken down to the police station and their fancy lawyer was right behind them. They were very distraught and couldn't believe that their youngest had been kidnapped. They tried to blame me. Said I must have done something to him because I wasn't going to win the custody case. Made it seem like I had a questionable lifestyle that was rubbing off on Danny and now, he was in danger because of me.

Their lawyer tried to file for a restraining order against me because of it. Thankfully, Jay was all over it and got it shut down before the request even made it into the courthouse. My parents were released after their interview. Detective Hollingsworth said it would be better to leave them in play. They might contact someone or lead us to the camp.

Ever since they were released from custody, though, it'd been one shitshow after the next.

They were trying everything they could to get me discredited and blame all of this on me. There had been multiple court requests, more than I ever thought possible with it only being four days, truly three when the first request came in.

Jay said it was to be expected. They were behind Danny's kidnapping and they were trying to keep us busy so we couldn't look for him. Judge Wilson was on our side and he was shutting it down right away, saving Jay time from having to go back and forth to court.

Rumors were running wild right now in town. This was the biggest case the town had seen in decades, quite possibly in the century.

Kidnappings didn't happen here.

Murders and horrible crimes didn't happen in our somewhat small town.

The press from towns all the way up to Baltimore were coming down here every day to cover the case. They pushed for interviews, but I refused to talk to anyone. Jay said it would be best if I stayed quiet, that the evidence would speak for itself. I couldn't let myself get distracted and he was right.

My parents, on the other hand, were loving all of the attention. They were playing the role perfectly, but that was fine. I knew the truth and I was going to make sure everyone did. Once Danny was safe, once the arrests were made, then I would tell the world exactly what type of people the Smythes were.

"We got em!" Sebastian called out as he ran into the room with his cell phone in his hand.

My heart shot right up into my throat. This could very well be the moment that I had been waiting four days for.

The moment when someone would finally tell me where my baby brother was.

"Where?" Damien demanded.

"Brooks finally led Masoc to the camp. He's got an anchor down and taking photos of all the kids and adults. He texted me the address. It's about an hour out. He hasn't seen Danny, yet, but he has seen kids as young as twelve there."

"How do we know it's the camp and not something else?" Detective

Hollingsworth asked. I hated him for asking, but I understood why he did.

"It's a factory-like building with a fifteen foot high fence with barbed wire at the top all around the property. The kids he has seen are all wearing beige clothing, and they have their heads down. They are supervised by an adult as they are guided from one area to the next. It's completely isolated, there's no way for them to leave, and even if they do, it's hours away from any help. This is the camp," Sebastian said, with full confidence as he went over to the map and circled the location.

"I'll call my Captain. It's going to take some time, though, to get the manpower to raid the camp. We'll have to call in help from Baltimore. We don't have anywhere near enough manpower for something like this," Detective Hollingsworth said as he pulled out his phone.

My stomach hit the floor.

No, we couldn't wait longer.

Danny might not have longer.

All I could think about these past four days was the story Jay told me about his own experiences in the camp.

Danny would know I was looking for him, that I would come for him, but what if that wasn't good enough?

What if something happened and he couldn't handle it and he took his life?

We couldn't waste more time.

I had to get to him.

Now.

"Call your Captain to update him, but we don't have to wait for manpower. I've had a team of federal agents ready and waiting in the next town over for when we have something. They've also been running financials on all of the possibles and everyone Brooks has come into contact with. They'll be good to go within the hour to meet us there," Damien stated.

"All right, I'll let him know. We'll need social workers there, as well," Detective Hollingsworth said with the phone to his ear.

"I'll call Travis Manning and explain what we have. His background check came back clean. He'll be able to get us a team of social workers for the children. I'll also put a call in to some lawyer friends of mine in Baltimore. They'll come down and make sure all of the children are in safe homes," Jay added.

It seemed like everyone had

connections with people. I didn't have any connections to offer up, not unless we broke down on the side of the road. Just another reason why Jay and me were not a good match. He was all book smart and I was street smart. I knew opposites attract, but maybe this was the universe's way of telling me that we shouldn't be together. I mean, I finally lost my virginity to a man and that very night my brother got kidnapped. If that's not a sign, I don't know what is.

"Perfect," Detective Hollingsworth said, and then, he moved away to speak with his Captain.

The others got on their phones and started to get into contact with who they needed. All I could do was sit there waiting for when someone would finally tell me we were getting into a car. I just wanted to be on the road. I knew they had to make sure everything was organized and ready for the raid on the camp. I knew there were more children at risk than just Danny, but that didn't make it any easier.

Jay came over to me and he bent down so we were eye level, placing his hand on my knee as he spoke.

"It's gonna be okay. We know where he is and, now, we can get him and all of the other kids safe. When we get there, we have to let the Feds handle the raid and clear the place of any threats before we can go in."

"Fine, but if I see Danny, I'm not waiting for anyone."

There was no way I was going to let Danny slip through my fingers, federal agents or not.

"If he is outside of the gates then okay, but you can't go in otherwise. The Feds need to be able to focus on securing the men responsible and not having to worry about a civilian going rogue and heading inside. You could get any of those kids hurt if you do. As hard as it is, I need you to let them do their job."

His voice was calm and gentle, but I hated it all the same. It wasn't so much that he was telling me, but *what* he was telling me that had me upset. I didn't want to have to wait. All I had been doing for four days was waiting and, now, I was waiting again to be able to hug Danny and make sure he was okay. I hated it, but arguing with Jay would be pointless.

I simply gave a nod and Jay stood

back up to answer his phone. For the next hour, I sat there waiting for the phone calls to stop so we could get in the car. Finally, after what felt like an eternity we were heading for the car and I was finally on the road to saving Danny.

***

I couldn't stand still. Having to stand off on the sidelines while a group of men stormed into the camp to free the children, free my brother, was nerve wracking and a lot harder than I expected.

I wasn't a violent person, but I could hold my own in a fight. I was a firm believer in being able to defend yourself in a fight. You didn't have to win, you just had to be good enough to survive long enough to get away.

I had done a bit of training with Danny, but I didn't want to push it with him. He was so smart, a lot smarter than me, and I knew he would use his mind to get him out of difficult situations. He didn't need fists to defend himself. I thought I had been doing the right thing by only teaching him a few basic maneuvers, but now I was questioning that. Maybe, I should have taught him more, taught him better so he was ready for a life or death situation. Maybe, if I had, he wouldn't have been taken and we wouldn't be standing here. All of these *what ifs* were pointless, I knew that, but I couldn't stop my mind from asking them.

"They're coming out with some of the children," Jay said as he put his phone back into his pocket.

I knew he had been keeping in touch with Damien, who had been allowed to go in with the Feds. Why, I didn't know nor care right now. I just wanted to get eyes on Danny. That was all that mattered to me, right now.

I couldn't stop my finger from taping against my leg as I waited minute after minute to finally start seeing some of the kids that were trapped in this hell. I watched as Detective Hollingsworth started to bring some of the children out and the group of social workers and lawyers that had arrived made their way over to them.

There were also paramedics here to bring the children to the hospital. Everyone was going to be getting examined to ensure they were healthy and not injured. As each child walked out of the gates, I was scanning them to see if I could find the only child I truly cared about at this moment. Closer to the back of the line was when I finally felt like I could get a breath in.

"Danny," I said softly, before I started to run toward him. I didn't care who was in my way. They were either going to move, or I would push them down.

"Thad!" Danny yelled out as he saw me and started to run toward me.

The second he was close enough, I wrapped my arms around him and instantly we were both crying. Just being able to feel him safe in my arms again, the whole world disappeared. He was safe, he was finally safe, and that was all that I cared about.

"It was so bad," He cried and it broke

my heart even more.

I couldn't even imagine what he had been through, what he had seen, in the past four days. I hated that I couldn't take that away from him, that I couldn't have saved him from this. I would have easily traded places with him in a heartbeat, if I could.

"I'm so sorry. You're safe now. I promise you'll never have to go through something like that again."

I didn't care what I had to do. I would steal him and go on the run if that is what it took. He was never going to go through something like that ever again. I was never going to allow our parents to get anywhere near him again. I continued to hold onto him, but I could feel his body trembling and I worried about what trauma his body had been through. He needed to get looked at.

"Come on, you need to get looked at by the medics," I said as I rubbed my hand along his back.

"In a minute, I just need another minute, please," he begged as the tears continued to pour down his face, soaking my shirt.

"Okay, as long as you need," I easily agreed.

He needed to get looked at and he would need to speak with a therapist. He had a long road to go before he recovered from all of this, but we could wait to start. If he needed me to hold him, for now, that was exactly what I was going to do.

CHAPTER FOURTEEN

Jay

WATCHING THE AMBULANCE drive away with Thad and Danny in it was a lot harder than I expected it to be. I wanted to be there with them. I wanted to be able to hold Thad's hand and be there while Danny was examined. To be able to comfort Thad while he was going through all that, waiting to hear about the abuse his brother had suffered, was something my body was screaming at me for.

I hated that I couldn't have protected either of them from this. I had always been a protector. It was ingrained into me. I had always protected the small kids in the foster homes. I always protected Chris. At least, to the best of my ability. I protected the children that came across my desk looking for a safe home to live in. The one time in my life I had failed a client and this had been the result.

I knew, logically, it was a good thing that we had been able to discover this camp and get it shut down. Still, that didn't make the circumstances around how we discovered the camp any less painful. I would have much preferred to find its location through the investigation without having another child taken through the gates of Hell.

Letting out a sigh, I turned my attention to said gates. I needed to go inside. I had to try and find the others and see if there was anything I could do. I was still a lawyer and there were a lot of children still being brought out and checked over by paramedics.

I'd never expected to ever have to go back to a place like this in my life. When I ran away at sixteen, I swore it would be for good. That the walls that housed so many horrors would be behind me and I would never have to face them again. Turned out, that was a lie. The horrors lived in my head and it took almost dying from drug abuse for me to be able to see it.

Standing out there was not going to help any of those children. I had to suck it up and do it, memories or not. They could only hurt me if I allowed them to, and I was far too old to allow them that type of power.

Sucking in a deep breath, I convinced my feet to move and headed through the gates to make my way to where I knew Damien was inside. I did my best not to look around. I didn't need to trigger any memories that were already threatening to break out of their box.

It was easy to feel the cold air in the facility. Camp leaders always keep the air conditioning on low so it didn't encourage the children to remove their shirts around each other. The walls were bare, void of anything that could trigger a child and their unnatural urges. The doors to the rooms were all half open and I knew that was from the feds going through and sweeping each room to ensure no one was missed. I kept my gaze firmly forward so I wouldn't have to see the horrors within the rooms.

I saw Damien speaking with Travis for a moment, before Travis gave a nod and headed off. I couldn't help but notice Damien looking after him as he walked away.

"See something you like?" I asked with a smirk once I was close enough.

"Something seems off with him."

"He seemed fine to me. He's probably just stressed with the shitstorm we just dropped in his lap."

Travis seemed normal to me from the very small conversations that we'd had. He liked Thad over his parents, and that was good enough for me.

"Hm. How's the kid?"

"They just left in an ambulance to get checked out. He was only here for four days, so I don't think there's anything physically wrong with him. The other kids that I've seen weren't looking too good."

Some of the kids looked wrecked, like they had been locked away in a dark hole for years. I worried that it was actually true. That they were going to find a hole with chains that would give a serial killer thrills.

"Some of the rooms were pretty rough. A crime scene team is on their way down from Baltimore to start processing."

"Good. You never told me you had connections with the feds." He never told me anything. It was such a fun game we were playing. Not.

"I've met people along the way. Shouldn't you be getting to the hospital, too?"

"I wanted to make sure all of the children were taken care of. I didn't want to leave and then you needed an extra hand."

Of course, I wanted to be in my car heading back to town, to the hospital, but I also knew that Danny wasn't the only victim. I had to make sure everyone was looked after first, before I ran off.

"We've got my people on the way. Go, be with them. You'll be useless here, anyway, with your mind back on them."

Ouch.

He was going to pay for the useless comment, even if it might be a bit true.

I gave a nod toward where Sebastian and Detective Hollingsworth were currently standing and talking.

"They seem to be hitting it off. They've been getting closer and closer over the past four days. Detective Hollingsworth seems to be interested in him."

That wasn't just a dig to get back at him, either. They really did seem to be getting closer. I had no idea if either of them was gay, but I could assume based on the lingering looks and unnecessary touches over the past four days.

They were both very attractive men and they could make a good couple. The problem would be whatever the secret that the brothers were hiding. If it was bad, it could ruin any hope they had at a real relationship.

"They're just doing their job," Damien

said with an edge to his voice, and I knew he was not in the mood for that conversation. I didn't know who was the older brother, but my money was on Damien.

"Sure. If you don't need me, then I'll head to the hospital and start helping out there." I moved closer so only he would hear me as I spoke into his ear. "Oh, and try and prevent your brother from getting ravaged in a conversion camp. That's not very romantic."

I moved out of the way fast enough to avoid the elbow that was aiming for my gut. I let out a chuckle as I headed back out. I was going to miss the epic sex that we shared together, but I was glad that Damien and me would still be able to be friends. He was a good man and hopefully one day I would finally get to discover what his story actually was.

***

To say that the hospital was a mad house would be an understatement. We really should have given them a heads up of what was to come, but we didn't think about that part. All we had been focused on was getting to the kids and getting them out. We didn't really think about the flood it would put on the hospital.

We were bringing all of the kids back to town because we didn't know where else to bring them. There were just over two hundred children in that camp, all between the ages of eleven and seventeen. From what little information we were able to gather from them once we got them free, they came from multiple States. It was a logistics nightmare and something that Travis and myself would have to work through. It was going to be a long process with a lot of sleepless nights, but it would all be worth it if we could save these kids from any more pain.

I made my way through the hospital to try and find Thad. I knew they would be down in the emergency department with everyone else that was coming in. The place was a mess and I would need to jump in soon to try and help them get organized. Right now, I needed to find Thad and Danny and make sure they were still okay before I got back to work.

After five minutes, I finally located them. I didn't find Danny, but Thad was standing outside an examination room so I could assume Danny was inside. I knew from personal experience that some of the abuse, or *conditioning,* as they called it, was sexual in nature. Some camps believed in doing it after the first few months and others believed it was the quickest way to cure the gayness out of a boy. None of it was fun and all of it involved pain.

Generally, they restrained the child to a chair, naked, placed electrodes to their genitals, and played heterosexual porn and then homosexual porn. If they got hard while watching the gay porn, the mentor would hit the button and give them a shock to make them go soft.

It was designed to rewire their brain to think that getting hard while watching two guys would only cause them pain. Therefore, they wouldn't get hard when watching guys.

That would then be taken to another level of being touched by another man and the process would be repeated until they couldn't get hard for fear of the pain associated with it.

It was torture, there was no other word for it, and I prayed that Danny didn't have to go through that. I had escaped before they had tried any of that on me. I suspected Chris had endured it and that was why he killed himself.

"Hey, Babe, how is he?" I asked, once I was close enough.

"He seems okay. Tired and dehydrated, but he seemed okay on the way over. The doctor wanted to examine him alone."

I could tell he wasn't happy about being out here and having his brother in there alone, but it would be better for

Danny to be alone, right now. Still, that didn't make it any easier on Thad.

"I know it's hard, but he's safe, now. He was only there for four days, thankfully. Not that it wouldn't be traumatic, but it could have been a lot worse. Some of the older kids, sixteen, seventeen, had been there since they were twelve."

"I couldn't imagine. What the hell is wrong with people? It's not like they were all serial killers sent to a reform camp. They love guys, so what? Where's the inexcusable crime in that?" He was genuinely confused and pissed.

I was like that when I was younger, too. I still didn't get why.

"I don't know. Old beliefs play a huge role in it. It's not something that can change overnight. It's something that we all have to work on and keep standing up for. It took women twenty-nine years before they were finally able to vote. It's a hard and long fight, but it's a fight worth having so this never happens again."

"I know. I just feel so useless, right now. I can't be in there with him and I can't help anyone out here."

"The hardest thing is to do nothing sometimes. It's a mess around here and I'll have to jump in, soon, to try and get things organized. There are more children on their way in. I'm going to be helping Travis get everyone into proper foster homes and try to find a suitable relative that they could live with. Some of the older children, I'll take their case on for emancipation and they can try to put everything behind them. We'll have to work with a therapist, or a herd of them, for everyone. Danny should speak with someone, too."

"I'm going to talk to him about it later. He has to talk to someone about all of it. Once the doctor is finished with him, he has to be interviewed by a detective before he can leave. My place is still a crime scene, too. I gotta find a hotel room for the night, or the next couple of nights, until we can get into the apartment again."

"You don't need to get a room, Sweetheart. You guys can stay with me."

The offer was a lot easier than I expected. I had long given up trying to convince myself that I didn't love him. I had fallen for him. Way too easily and way too soon, but my heart wanted what it wanted, and I was done trying to ignore it. There was no point in ignoring it. I was in love with him and I was going to embrace every aspect of it.

I could tell he was surprised by the offer and uncertain. It wasn't like we had a conversation about what we were. We'd had it in the beginning, about just being friends with benefits, but not since. I had no idea if he wanted more. I was really hoping he wanted more and it wasn't one sided. I don't think I could handle unrequited love.

"Are you sure? Wouldn't that be crossing a line between us?"

"The line was crossed a long time ago, Thad. At first, I was a bit freaked out by it, but now I'm really happy that we did cross the line. I know it's still early days between us, but I'm madly in love with you. I don't want to be just friends with benefits. I want to date you. I want something real. I want complicated and messy. I want you and everything that comes with it."

I was going have a heart attack while I waited for him to respond to that verbal vomit. At least, I was standing in an ER for it. If he didn't feel the same way, the floor beneath me better open up and swallow me whole. I wasn't going to be able to handle it if he didn't want to be with me, if he didn't want to date me.

"I love you, too," he said, and flashed the first real smile I had seen on him in four days.

"You do?"

He loved me.

He actually loved me back.

Holy shit.

"Of course I do. Jay, you're amazing

and very easy to fall in love with. I know I don't have any experience in the relationship department, and I'm going to make rookie mistakes, but I love you and I want a real relationship with you."

"I don't have any experience, either, so we can make those rookie mistakes together. I love you, Baby," I said, before I pulled him in for a kiss.

Thad easily welcomed the kiss and pressed his lips against mine. As badly as I wanted to deepen the kiss and show him exactly how much I loved him, we couldn't. We were currently standing in the hospital with traumatized children around us. The last thing they needed was two guys going at it in the hallway.

I reluctantly pulled back after a moment and spoke.

"I should start helping with the other

victims. Are you okay on your own?"

"Yeah, I'll be fine. I'm gonna wait until I can sit with Danny. You go and help. They need you more than I do, right now."

"I'll come by and check in on you. Text me if you get out of here before me and I'll give you my spare key. The guest bedroom has clean sheets and there's not much food in the fridge. We should probably order something."

"I'll ask the doctor what he can have. He said he hadn't eaten since he was taken."

Assholes.

"It's normally simple food. Let me know what he says, and if you need any help with the detective, just call me and I'll come be with you guys for it."

"Okay, you go and help them. I'll be

fine. We'll be fine."

He sounded more confident than when I had arrived, so I gave him one last kiss before I headed over to the nurses' station to see where I could jump in. It was going to be a long day, but at the end of it, my reward would be curling up with Thad in bed and that was more than worth it.

EPILOGUE

Thad

IT HAD BEEN an insane two weeks.

Everything had been going so slow for months and the second we arrived at the hospital, it was like someone had put jet fuel in the car. Within twenty-four hours of getting Danny back safe, my parents had been arrested and I was awarded sole custody of Danny.

We had also been given restraining orders and no contact orders toward both of our parents. They were up on multiple charges and facing up to seven years in federal prison. From what Jay had said, they would most likely plead out to avoid jail time, but part of that plea deal could be the both of them terminating their parental rights so we would never have to worry about them trying to fight in court for Danny again.

They would also have to pay millions in restitution for the emotional and physical trauma that Danny endured. I didn't want any money from them, but that money would be placed in an account for Danny to use for his education or his life. The only reason I would entertain any money from them would be because it would free up

Danny from financial pressures. He wouldn't have to struggle and work through college, or through life, while he was healing from what they had done.

He had been different in the past two weeks. He was quiet and kept to himself. He stayed in his room and didn't go out with his friends or do his volunteer work since he got back home.

I couldn't blame him. It was a lot to process and to deal with. Even if he didn't go through any of the torture that place created, he would have seen it from others going through it.

I had managed to find us another place that we could move into at the end of the month. We both didn't feel safe or secure in the apartment after what happened and the fresh start would be good for Danny. At least, I hoped it would be.

Jay had been amazing. He had allowed us to stay as long as we wanted. We could have stayed until we moved into the new apartment, but I wanted Danny to start having a bit of a normal life again. His therapist said it would be best for him to get back to his life.

Still, Jay didn't complain about me sleeping with Danny when he had a hard time at night. When the nightmares got too bad, and Danny woke us up in the middle of the night with his screams, Jay joined us and offered any comfort he could.

I had sat down with Danny before we stayed at Jay's that first night and told him I was gay and that me and Jay were dating. He had taken it very well, not that I was too worried about him being weird with it. The three of us were building a family together, in a sense, and it felt good to know that my brother liked Jay and they would be able to build their own bond.

Jay had been running himself ragged over the past two weeks. He was one of ten family lawyers that were working the cases of the camp victims, over two hundred of them. He had twenty-two new cases of children between the ages of eleven and seventeen.

He had a few that were easier. The older boys were a perfect and simple case of emancipation and he was getting their paperwork completed. The younger kids were more complicated. Some had parents from out of state, so he had to work with other law enforcement in their home state.

Travis was working with social workers from other states, as well, for all of the children. It was a mess, because the kids couldn't go back home to their parents, but some didn't have other relatives that could take them or they could trust with them. They had to be placed in foster homes, but it was a logistics nightmare with them being from different states. They had to try and figure out what state the child would be in and what foster home.

Both Travis and Jay didn't want just any foster home for the kids. The last thing those kids needed, was to be abused in a foster home after what they had been through.

There was one boy that Jay had taken a special interest in. Max. He was seventeen and turning eighteen in six weeks. He had been in the camp since he was eleven years old, almost seven years of torture and brainwashing. Max's parents were extremely strict and held bigoted views.

When Max was eleven, his father walked in on him playing dress up with his four year old sister. His father had assumed he was gay because he was wearing heels and a dress without any confidence issue. Max didn't even know if he was gay before he was thrown into that camp. He was just a good older brother playing with his kid sister, but his parents didn't care.

Now, he was an extremely messed up seventeen year old who had no idea what his sexuality was or how to stop feeling like he was dirty.

Jay had almost broken down when he

told me about him and I knew Max's story was going to stay with him forever.

When it looked like Max was going to be placed in a mental facility because no foster or group home wanted him, Jay had decided he couldn't sit quietly by. He took him in. He was still going to get him emancipated, but he made it clear that when he turned eighteen, he didn't have to leave. Now, he lived with Jay and went each day for intensive therapy to try and remove the brainwashing that he underwent. The fact that Jay took Max in only made me love him even more.

That was why today I was going to finally be brave enough to experience my last first sexual experience with Jay.

Today, I was going to bottom.

I broke apart from the kiss and looked up at Jay. He was currently between my legs and we had been enjoying a rare moment alone with each other. Both Danny and Max were in therapy for the next hour. We hadn't had much time to ourselves over the past two weeks, but I wasn't upset about it. We were both busy with our responsibilities and I knew it would take a bit before our lives went back to a normal steady flow.

"I want you," I said against his lips.

"I want you," Jay said back to me, but I knew he didn't quite understand what I meant.

"No, I want you in me this time. I want to feel you."

Jay pulled back slightly before he spoke. "You sure?"

"Yes, I've been experimenting with a toy."

Jay moaned at the images I was

certain were going through his mind right now. He quickly reached over to the bedside table and pulled out the lube. I knew he had been wanting me to try bottoming and see how I liked it, but I hadn't been ready yet. He had been very sweet with waiting and not pressuring me, but I knew he was very excited about this.

He kissed his way down my neck and body as he coated three fingers in lube. He easily took my dick into his mouth as he worked his first finger inside of me.

I had experimented with myself so I knew what to expect and I knew any slight discomfort would be pleasure soon enough. I focused on the feeling of his mouth on me and when his fingers hit my prostate, I was arching off the bed and moaning. I loved that feeling and I knew Jay was going to make me love it even more.

Once I was ready, Jay was pulling his fingers out and removing his mouth from me.

"You sure?" he asked with a burning desire in his eyes.

"Hell yes."

Jay placed his hands on my legs and brought them up to his shoulders. The angle would give me the most pleasure possible. He went slow, at first, as he pushed his tip inside of me. Once again, I knew it would hurt for a minute and then it would feel amazing. He went slowly until he was finally balls deep inside of me. He paused, though, to allow me to adjust to his size. He was bigger than the toy I had been using, but he felt amazing.

"You okay?" he asked.

"You feel so good. Bigger than the toy I've been using. You can move. I'm good."

I wanted nothing more than to feel him moving. I knew before he even moved that I was just like him. A switch. I knew the fact that we were both switches was only going to make our sex life all the more exciting.

He slowly pulled out almost all of the way before he pushed back in. He went slow at first, but once he started to pick up his pace, I was instantly moaning and writhing beneath him.

The position we were in allowed him to go so deep, deeper than any toy I had been able to get, and it felt astronomically amazing. My whole body was on fire and it was pooling right in my stomach. I was close already.

The repeated hits on my sweet spot were making me see stars and the way his hips picked up, I knew he was right there with me. The connection of having him in me was intoxicating and I wanted more of it.

I fell over the cliff first, but Jay was right behind me. The feel of him pulsing inside of me had me coming a bit more. I thought being a top felt good, but bottoming felt just as amazing. I knew I could easily become addicted to this, addicted to this man, and for the first time I was perfectly fine with it.

Jay moved my legs down before he collapsed down on top of me slightly. He made sure all of his weight wasn't on me so I could breathe. We were both breathing hard and my whole body was tingling and I loved it.

"We gotta do that more," I said, flashing him a big, goofy smile.

He gave a warm and rich chuckle at that. "As much as you want. In any combination."

I turned so I could look at him as I spoke. "I love you."

"I love you too, Babe."

He moved in and softly kissed me and at that very moment the world could have ended and I knew I would be okay. When all of this started, I never expected that my life would change so much.

To think that I could have missed out on all of this if I had picked a different lawyer for my court case. Maybe the world put us together for this very reason.

Whatever magic was at play in the

universe, I was damn glad that it decided we needed the other. I couldn't imagine my life without Jay and I was looking forward to everything the future held for us.

Thank you for reading Rescue, book four in From the Edge.

If you enjoyed Rescue, please return to your retailer and leave a review. Even a few words can mean the world to an author. Plus it helps other readers like you find our work, too.
Share the love! ;)

Turn the page to read a preview from Hidden, the next book in the series.

PREVIEW

Eli

THESE PAST TWO months have not been easy on me. When I was trapped in the conversion camp, all I could think about was escaping the hell. After two and a half years, I never expected to be able to get out before my eighteenth birthday, which was a week ago, but I was finally free.

Craig Brooks, the evil piece of work who ran the camp, had finally made a fatal mistake by taking the wrong boy. A boy who had a brother that loved him very much and refused to allow him to be taken to a camp that would brainwash and condition him.

Now, over two hundred of us were finally free from the camp and it'd been shut down. The life of hell was over... or so I'd thought.

Unfortunately, the true reality of my situation has finally hit me. My freedom didn't come with leaving those walls. I was still trapped, but instead of cement walls that kept me in, it was my own mind.

Everyday was a challenge for me to be able to function. I was struggling with sleeping. I was struggling with being around people. I was struggling with being touched. I was a mess, and I was trapped in that hell in my own head.

So many of the other guys got to go somewhere. They got to go to a family member or to a foster home where they were safe. But me, my aunt was supposed to come and get me, but she never showed.

People didn't know that, but no one really asked, either. They just assumed she came and got me like she said she would. Only, when she didn't show, I was left with nothing all over again. I had no family. Well, I had my brother, but that was different. That wasn't a loving adult who would be there for me. I was still older than him, so it was on me to try and take care of him.

Which is what brought me to the

mall. I was determined to put it all behind me and get a job. I didn't have an address, but I thought maybe I could talk my way around that one.

What I didn't expect was how I would react in the mall. I was fine, at first, but then people started to bump into me. My heart started to pound in my chest, my chest got tight, and breathing became difficult, and then the world around me started to morph into something different.

Suddenly, I wasn't in the mall.

I was back in that room.

The torture room.

I was strapped down to the chair, naked, and they were shocking me with a cattle prod every time a scene from a gay porno played on the screen. I wasn't stupid, I knew what they were trying to do. They wanted my mind to connect homosexuality with pain. They wanted to rewire my brain. But what they didn't expect was for me to hold onto the memories of all of the pleasure I got from messing around with my boyfriend before I was trapped here.

"Homosexuality is a disease. The only way to cure you, is to remove it from your body," Ralph, one of the men who worked at the camp, barked once again before he pushed the cattle prod into my side.

I had tried to stop screaming when they did it—they seemed to enjoy the screams—but no matter how hard I tried, I couldn't keep the screams in. The pain was always horrific, no matter how many times it had happened to me. They knew where to push the prod to inflict the most pain.

I knew the electrical burns would stay for weeks, but it wouldn't stop them from strapping me down to this chair. I did my best to try and block it all out. To block out the vile and cruel words they were spewing at me. I knew what would come next. Once they were done showing me how painful being gay was, they would take it to the next level.

Jessica.

A prostitute who got paid to sleep with the guys here in the camp.

I had never had sex with her, but she would give me oral and I would close my eyes and pretend that she was a guy. Sometimes, in the beginning, I could get hard. But recently, I couldn't even get hard anymore. That only made it go longer, because they wouldn't stop until I finally shot my load or hours went by and there was clearly no point.

I was always caught between hating the pain and hating her touching me. At first, I hated when she touched me. I preferred to be tortured over being touched. But as time went on, I would prefer her touching me over the pain. I hated it, but at least it didn't hurt. Physically, anyway.

"Stop resisting," a male voice said beside my ear.

I was suddenly on the ground with an unknown burly man on top of me. I couldn't see much, just random shoes and unrecognizable voices.

I wasn't in the torture room any longer.

I was in the mall.

My hands were pulled behind my back and I felt the cold metal of handcuffs as they were snapped tight around both wrists. I was being arrested, but I had no idea why.

"Get off of me, I didn't do anything," I said as I tried to get free. I didn't want him touching me and I didn't want my hands cuffed. I needed my hands free. I had to be able to defend myself. My heart pounded in my chest and bile crept up my throat.

"You're under arrest for destruction of property. Get up," the police officer said as he pulled my arms and I forced my body to move to stand.

I had no idea what he was talking about. I didn't destroy anything. Once I was standing, he started to walk me through the mall. It didn't take long for me to see that the place I was about to apply at, their whole storefront was destroyed. There was broken glass everywhere and, apparently, I was to blame for it. I didn't know why, though. I couldn't remember anything after my chest had become tight and I felt like I couldn't breathe.

Could I really have done that?

The officer placed me into the back of his squad car and I had no choice but to sit there as he drove me to the station. I had never been arrested before, so I had no idea what was going to happen or how it all worked. I couldn't bring myself to ask any questions, though. I stayed silent the whole short ride and once we stopped, he pulled me out and guided me into the station.

I could feel everyone's eyes on me as he guided me over to one of the two holding cells in the station. The one was empty and the other had ten guys already in it. When he guided me over to that one, my heart started to pound, I felt heat rush through my entire body, and it got hard for me to breathe again. It was in that moment that I decided to break my silence.

"Please, don't put me in that one."

I didn't care if it sounded like I was begging, I couldn't be locked in there with that many people. It was too small and too crowded. If I was going to be stuck here until morning, I couldn't do it in that cell. Thankfully, the police officer seemed to take pity on me and he brought me over to the empty cell. He gently removed my cuffs as he spoke.

"I'll be right back with some paperwork."

I couldn't contain the flinch at the

sound of the cell door being closed behind me. I went over to the farthest corner in the cell and sat down on the bench, bringing my legs up against my chest as tightly as I could.

I had been trapped in cells before, but they were to isolate and torture you in. Some were smaller. A lot smaller. One I was kept in wasn't even big enough for me to lay flat in. I normally passed out from lack of oxygen before anyone pulled me out. I didn't do well in rooms like this. I didn't do well anywhere, but I was trying. I guess I don't get a point for that.

I'm not sure how long I sat there alone before the cell door was opening and the officer was back. He had a clipboard, which I knew contained his paperwork, and a water bottle and a sandwich. He walked over to the bench and sat down just a bit away from me. He placed the water bottle and sandwich down in front of me as he spoke.

"I thought maybe you might be hungry. My name is Detective Roland Wright. Can I have your name?"

"Eli Edwards," I said, not touching the offered food or water. I knew better than that. Anything could be drugged. Anyone could want something in return for it. It was just better not to eat it, even if I hadn't eaten all week.

"Thank you. I am going to fill out this paperwork and then take you down to the courthouse. Judge Wilson will see you and let you know what he is going to expect you to do and then you can go home."

"Wait, what?" I asked confused.

I had been arrested. I didn't know

much about the law, but I did know that I should be stuck here until tomorrow and then I'd be taken in front of a judge to see if I could be granted bail, something I wouldn't be able to afford, anyway, and then, because I couldn't pay, I'd be stuck in jail.

Why was everything moving so fast?

"I saw your wrists, the scars," he said gently.

I pulled my sleeves down to make sure my wrists were covered. I hated the scars, but there was nothing I could do about them. It was from the restraints.

"You are one of the camp survivors."

"Most call us victims." I hated that word but that was what everyone called us.

A victim.

For some reason, that made me feel

worse.

"You're a survivor, Eli. You survived a level of hell that I can't even begin to understand. But you aren't a victim, because you got out. You are here and fighting for your life back." He offered me a warm smile. His words were kind, but I wasn't sure if that was what I was doing, fighting. It felt more like I was drowning.

"And to answer your question, what happened to you today was called a flashback. You didn't mean to cause damage. We know that. You didn't know what you were doing while you were in that fugue state. I've called Judge Wilson and the store owner and explained your situation. Judge Wilson is holding an emergency hearing where he will tell you what you need to do to get the arrest off your record. What you went through, Eli, you are going to struggle and you don't deserve to be punished for something that is out of your control."

I was trying my best not to let his words affect me, but it was a losing battle. All I could do was focus on not allowing the tears that built up in my eyes to escape. I couldn't remember the last time someone was this nice to me.

He didn't talk down to me like I was a little kid, like the doctors or nurses did in the hospital. He talked to me like I was an adult.

An adult who was hurting.

He didn't have to be kind. He wasn't obligated to be. He could have easily tossed me away in the other cell and left me there until morning, but he didn't. He was genuinely being nice and I couldn't for the life of me remember what that felt like.

"Thank you."

He deserved to have so much more than that, but that was all I could come up with to say. Thankfully, he understood exactly what words I couldn't get out.

We spent the next hour going over the paperwork and I offered what information I could about the outburst. I didn't really remember any of it, but I told him what I did remember and that seemed to be good enough.

Once the paperwork was done, he took me out of the cell, thankfully, without the cuffs, and took me out to his car. He helped me climb into the front seat, another surprise considering I was supposed to be in the back seat.

We drove in comfortable silence the

short distance to the courthouse. Once there, I followed Officer Wright as he went through the procedures to get in and get me taken down to the proper courtroom where Judge Wilson would be. It all happened pretty quickly and he even stayed with me as I was in the courtroom.

I stood as Judge Wilson walked into the room and made his way over to his bench. I really didn't know what to do at this point. I had only ever seen a few television shows and not really any of them had any courtroom scenes.

It wasn't often I was allowed to watch television growing up and then it wasn't allowed in the camp. There were a lot of entertainment things I missed out on.

Officer Wright instructed me to sit down as Judge Wilson spoke. I complied without question.

"Eli Edwards, it has been brought to my court that you caused damage to a store front at the mall. I have spoken with the store owner and there is ten thousand dollars in damage. Now, Detective Wright has informed me that you are one of the conversion camp survivors and that you were not aware of your actions at the time. You were apparently in the midst of a flashback and had no cognitive awareness of your actions. I have explained that to the store owners and they have agreed to drop the charges if you pay for the damages. They are going to give you two years to pay for it. If it is not paid by the end of two years, they will be well within their rights to file charges against you. Any questions?"

"No, Sir."

I couldn't believe this was happening. I wasn't going to be charged. I had no idea how I was going to ever be able to pay them back, but that was something for me to figure out another day. It didn't have to be today's issue.

"That is for the store owners. For me, for this court, I am also ordering you to have a mental health evaluation with a court ordered psychiatrist named Dr. Bailey. She will evaluate your mental state and provide you with any help you may need to prevent a situation like this from happening again. The first time is acceptable and understandable. However, you now know about this issue and you are expected to have it handled. Do you understand, Mr. Edwards?"

"Yes, Sir."

I had no idea what was wrong with me or why it was happening, but I could understand that I was only going to get this pass once. I didn't know how I felt about seeing a shrink, but if it was a requirement for me not to go to jail, I would be happy to do it.

I had no idea what this shrink would want from me or tell me was wrong with me, but maybe it would help. It wasn't just me I had to be worried about and take care of. If I was able to be better, then that was an avenue I needed to explore.

I just hoped this Dr. Bailey didn't decide to tell me I'm broken for good.

Watch for Hidden at your favorite online
retailer.

OTHER BOOKS BY EVIE

Federal Protection Agency
Mason
Rafe
Ryzen
Cooper
Noah
Damien
Sebastian
Gabe
Logan

Ruthless Empire
Courting Danger
Chasing Danger
Kissing Danger

Smokejumpers
Hawke
Cyrus
Jase
Gage
Jackson
Xavier

Jasper Springs
Cade
Dawson
Drew
Grayson
Riley
Mitch

From The Edge
Shattered
Runaway
Jaded
Rescue
Hidden
Tormented

Gray Vale Pack
His Fated Mate
His Wounded Warrior
His Healing Heart

ABOUT THE AUTHOR

Evie Riley is a prolific, neurodivergent author known for her captivating MM romance novels. She has gained a significant following and topped the LGBT+ action and adventure bestseller charts with her series.

Evie's writing style often explores dark and gritty themes where her men must overcome difficult obstacles in their search for love, but she has also ventured into sweeter small-town romances, incorporating tropes like enemies-to-lovers, friends-to-lovers, age-gap, and forced proximity. She is known for crafting engaging romantic suspense novels and has a knack for creating interconnected series worlds that keep readers invested.

Interestingly, Ms. Riley has hinted at exploring new genres, such as Alien Omegaverse Romance, in the future.

Outside of writing, she enjoys spending time at the beach and has a quirky personality, described by her partner as ranging from cute to deadly, depending on her blood-chocolate levels.

Evie spends her nights writing bad boys in love, and her days wrangling the sweet boys she loves.